Yankinton

Yankinton

RACHEL SHIHOR

TRANSLATED BY
SARA TROPPER AND ESTHER FRUMKIN

LONDON   NEW YORK   CALCUTTA

Seagull Books, 2020

© Rachel Shihor, 2020

First published in English translation by Seagull Books, 2020
English translation © Sara Tropper and Esther Frumkin, 2020

ISBN   978 0 8574 2 796 0

British Library Cataloguing-in-Publication Data
A catalogue record for this book is available
from the British Library

Typeset by Seagull Books, Calcutta, India
Printed and bound by Hyam Enterprises, Calcutta, India

Yankinton

In the long days of early summer, when the air had begun to shed its light, and the windowpanes, those not covered by grey blinds painted an opaque metallic colour, showed us behind them only hollow tubes of pierced air like the eyes of one half-blind who sees nothing but grey dots on wide, turbid surfaces, I would remember, even against my will, the endless Shabbat afternoons of my childhood when the idleness of the long day still lingered even when the waning light no longer allowed me to read the open book on my lap, and I drew near a window to catch the rapidly disappearing light, and the letters on the page, like the eyes of a sightless person, became pierced with dark air holes until they turned into isolated dots which I could no longer read, and I angled my hand holding the page to catch the last vestiges of light, but my momentary sense of victory melted away rapidly with the light itself and, though I could still make out my mother's and father's faces, the darkness made their features seem stricter.

In fact, there was nothing left to do but wait for the three stars to appear so that the light could shine forth from the electric lamps after my father would climb on the wooden stool, called the 'kitchen chair', and peer at the slits of the Shabbat timer—a clumsy brown box which hung in exactly the same place in each house: to the left of the entrance to the corridor, close to the ceiling. When the light came on, we were all still confused. We had difficulty identifying the features of the earlier faces which the darkness had gradually covered, causing us to forget them, and the light which appeared, its power demonstrating a certain violence, highlighted the new wrinkles and lines of those grown weary of a life of labour, lines added or deepened in the course of the day which had passed over us in boredom or at least moments of darkness which blanketed all of us while we were waiting for a new day to arrive.

Outside, the toads croaked. Not here, where we lived on the fourth floor of the tall building with porches on George Eliot Street, but a little farther east, along Melchett and Balfour Streets which cross Achad Ha'am Street and Rothschild Avenue, next to the home of Tzivoni, the child violinist whose parents forced him to play every morning for seven hours instead of attending school, and he would sit on the ground floor

of his parents' flat and play and his eyes would follow
the groups of pupils crowding around the large school
gate, still closed, to buy drinks and a new kind of candy
in the neighbouring kiosk. There, next to the low house
of Yossi Tzivoni, the road forked, one branch leading
into town and one leading to the field and the toads, as
it proceeded towards Yehuda Halevi Street and the back
of the Ten Dates football field. There, in a pool remaining
after a rainstorm, and facing low, dark clouds of swamp
mosquitoes, the toads croaked one after another and
their little bellies were full of mosquitoes.

Yehuda Halevi Street was the unmarked boundary
of the safe Tel Aviv, partially bourgeois and almost
entirely Ashkenazi. Beyond Yehuda Halevi Street and
up to Petach Tikvah Way and farther east, if that is even
possible, lived a different type of people: working people, small-business owners, garage owners and tax collectors, minor clerks in the municipality who were free
in the afternoon hours to work at a second job to aug-
ment their small salaries and would hang new curtains
in the houses of the nouveau riche and fill their mouths
with curtain hooks which forced them to keep their
mouths closed until they finished the work of hanging
the curtains, and more than one was injured, despite this
precaution, by the sharp end of a pin which wounded
his throat.

It was unthinkable for us to go alone to the Ten
Dates field, but in a group it became possible—in a
group and accompanied by a Scout leader not more than

a year or two older than us, but this arrangement nevertheless reassured our parents, and thus Yehuda Halevi Street became the border, beyond which dwelt the murky reality hard for us even to imagine, and certainly not see, since the presence of any teenager or adult caused it to withdraw immediately, but just because of that, its existence became more tangible to us than all those other things which declared the existence of a self-confident routine, like anything which slips away from us without our noticing. And during that period, the most precise bullets with the brightest trail were aimed and fired across this border, since the area from Yehuda Halevi Street eastwards was easily exposed to the gaze of an expert sniper who always stood at the top of the Hassan Bek tower in Jaffa, and his eyes followed us greedily. On such days, we were even more strictly forbidden to cross to the eastern side of the road unchaperoned. On other, quieter days, the prohibition eased up of its own accord, and we were allowed to go there, on the condition that we wore Scout uniforms, which we wore during Scout meetings anyway, and since the Scout meetings always took place under a counsellor's supervision, in the end we never crossed Yehuda Halevi Street to the east without being accompanied by someone thought to be more mature than us, supervision whose very futility blinded us from seeing the murky reality.

More than once, during the long summer days, Mrs Yankinton came to us for one of her visits. It was easy to predict this lady's visits to other people's houses, particularly our house, because her daughter was my close friend, but presumably it was not easy for Mrs Yankinton to go from house to house, between the homes of her daughter's friends, to ask if perhaps my Karni is here, so involved in playing that she forgot to come home? Certainly not easy during the burning hot summer days which lasted almost six months straight, but neither on stormy days when the blustery wind burnt the faces of the few passers-by and brought tears to their eyes. But climactic obstacles could not deter Mrs Yankinton while her beloved daughter's well-being, if not her very life, was at stake, even if the woman did not inhabit a particularly powerful body—she was not thin but her legs remained as slim as they had been in her youth, and she was proud of this. More than once she showed me her legs and asked with obvious satisfaction: My legs are beautiful, aren't they? Her concern for her daughter could never be assuaged, for this is a kind of thirst which gives a person strength. And like her, Mr Yankinton never ceased worrying about his daughter. It was enough for Karni to go on an innocent after-school visit to one of her many friends, since the two had agreed, while still at school, to meet on that day at five in the afternoon, and for her to neglect to inform her parents out of forgetfulness or weariness, to destroy Mr and Mrs Yankinton's peace of mind for all time, for if serenity is lost for even a moment, it will be found wanting for ever and nothing can restore it to its former state.

And thus, even when they discovered that their fears were ungrounded this time, Mr and Mrs Yankinton's hearts whispered that perhaps next time their fears would not be for nothing, and ultimately a day would surely come when their fears would not be for nothing, even if they would not live to witness such a day, and that small crack which was cut into their hearts for a moment, only to be smoothed over when the familiar footsteps were heard in the stairwell, would never knit together entirely; and like any repair, could gape open again on the day of the next disappearance, and thus Mr and Mrs Yankinton's souls would preserve the steadfast pain of people who suffer an irrevocable lack.

Mr Yankinton Hebraicized his name, as many residents of the land of Israel did in those days, after he heard his daughter singing the Song of the Hyacinth (in Hebrew, *yakinton*) as she had learnt it in nursery school. The song begins with the words, 'Nighttime, nighttime, the moon is watching,' and the father liked it immediately, finding in it a particular innocence which in his eyes was bound up with love for this land and love for his daughter, two loves entwined in his soul.

But in those days, proper Hebrew language was not in demand as much as it could have been, such that he accepted his baby daughter's pronunciation without checking it, and the flower which the moon watched remained *yankinton* in his ears and not *yakinton* as it is written in the dictionaries, and thus he recorded it at the Interior Ministry, and Mr Yankinton, when he lingered in his room crowded with books and manuscripts—all

Ze'ev Jabotinsky's speeches, waiting to be edited and readied for printing, as well as figurines and death masks of the leader who had passed away—he closed himself off from the outside world as long as his heart allowed him, up to the moment when he was overcome by a force which propelled him towards the window facing the street, where he opened the shutter which until then had darkened the interior of the high-ceilinged room, and thus he stood motionless, reading glasses in hand and gaze fixed on a random point across the street, along which passed hourly funeral processions of dead from the adjacent hospital. Thus he would stand, unable to do anything else, rooted to the spot while all his senses drowsed save that of sight, but this one remaining sense grew preternaturally alert and sharpened, even though it could not announce the joyful news of his daughter's return. It was necessary that she first return, but Mr Yankinton either refused to or perhaps could not admit this. His spirit could not accept that his daughter should be far away, lost, living her life without him in some unknown place of unknown character. Mr Yankinton was left therefore standing in his place, hidden in the shadows of the room, trying to give himself over to a moment in time which had not yet come to pass, in which he would again see the figure of his wife towing his daughter after her across the street, downcast and guilty but found.

Indeed, Mrs Yankinton went out a long time ago to look for her daughter. She was not yet really worried. At first she went out just because years of habit told her to do so before dusk fell. She reluctantly dressed in a grey skirt which she had bought in a workshop in Afula, where her brother the doctor lived, a worn blue georgette blouse, and had not even combed her hair properly when she passed the house of her childhood friend, Sonia Knizhnikov, with whom she'd emigrated from Russia to the Land of Israel when they were both very young. The worry in her heart was still not so great, a mere shadow which had yanked her from the house to the street, however this shadow was powerless to keep her from wondering what her friend was doing at that moment, and she decided first to climb the stairs of the grey building with white stripes decorating the windows and balconies surrounding it, where Sonia Knizhnikov lived with her only daughter Sofa and no husband to support her, and where perhaps as a surprise her daughter Karni might be waiting, playing all this time with the metal freight train belonging to Sofa, a girl whom life had taught to behave independently and even brashly, and she was two years older than Karni.

Karni had made such visits in the past when she passed the house while Sofa was standing in the window, and she would signal to her to come up, and Karni, though she had been sent by her mother to the corner grocery shop to bring a can of tuna for supper, immediately decided to postpone the purchase for the moment, 'for the tuna will not spoil in the meantime,' without obtaining her mother's permission, lest she not give it at all, so powerful was her desire to play with Sofa, climbed the stairs almost at a run, and put all other thoughts out of her head. And now Mrs Yankinton traced the same route herself, albeit with more effort, without lingering on the landings between floors, so powerful was her desire to see her friend Sonia and prove to herself that once more the two girls were playing together and Karni had again forgotten to ask her parents' permission before accepting her friend's invitation, and thus she rang the doorbell of the small flat.

Sofa was not home. She observed this immediately. Both rooms were empty, and dolls and upturned train cars were heaped up in Sofa's. Sonia, making the effort of the poor, spoilt her daughter with an abundance of toys not seen in the homes of her other friends. They were the kind of toys at which we used to gaze longingly in the display windows of expensive shops. And Sonia accompanied her friend to the door: Come another time for a cup of tea. The two friends understood each other without the need for many words. Mrs Yankinton got out the words with difficulty, 'I see that Karni is not here,' while Sonia Knizhnikov, who did not act emotionally, could not say: 'I love you and understand you as you are. Keep running. Even though you know what I think, that you are tormenting the girl, I will not say a word, and you will see that everything will work out in the end.' Sonia Knizhnikov did not say any of these things as she accompanied her friend to the door. And Mrs Yankinton, who thought in her heart how little Sofa's ways were unbridled and even wanton, how she was given no responsibility and her toys were always scattered and piled one on top of the other and therefore rapidly ruined, she too said not a word to her friend, even though she concluded to herself that she was really destroying her child this way and what would happen to her when she grew up, and she rapidly descended the narrow stairs to continue her visits.

Mrs Yankinton's visits followed a virtually fixed order, which she repeated when needed, when she was in great distress of body and spirit. Everywhere she went, Mrs Yankinton was welcomed and was not asked the purpose of her sudden visit, nor did she ask: Have you seen Karni? What she saw was enough, as her searching eyes combed many flats and hoped much, and each time taught themselves anew to do the impossible and stand before the emptiness. But as the series of visits lengthened, Mrs Yankinton's heart sank deeper, as she pretended she had all the time in the world and happened to show up here, out of boredom or a momentary sense of loneliness, to see how things were going, and would still smile when she spoke to people, but her face was unnaturally flushed and her heart beat unevenly.

In this way, after visiting many families along Mazeh Street, and passing along Ein Vered Alley, and ascending to the upper floor of Balfour's wide building, and ending up on Balfour Street but on the ground floor at the home of a family of bookkeepers, and before she decided to visit the Reins family on Mazeh Street, next to Yehuda Halevi Street, she suddenly arrived at our house. Karni was my close friend but she was not here. Mrs Yankinton understood that immediately. My mother offered her a cup of tea and she agreed, for her strength was nearly spent at this point and she needed to rest. Now she needed to chat lightly as though nothing was disturbing her tranquillity, and she did so, for she had developed expertise in these matters, and in doing so she had also learnt to hide the slight feeling of superiority which she always experienced in my parents' presence, who in her eyes were Jews from inferior stock, having come from 'East Europe', in her words, and she called them 'Eastjuden' in her heart, and the fact that they were 'a little ultra-Orthodox', as they described themselves to strangers, aroused in her a certain pity which mingled with the former feeling of superiority. Notwithstanding, my parents were still the parents of Karni's best friend, and Mrs Yankinton still hoped that perhaps Karni had considered, before returning home, stopping at our house for another short visit, and for that reason she agreed to a second cup of tea and continued speaking angrily—as one possessing extreme political awareness—of the harsh decrees which the government was imposing on the country's Jewish residents. After drinking two cups of tea and heaping criticism on the government, and after conversing with my parents as if they were her equals despite her roots in the ancient Russian homeland, and despite the time which had already passed and her daughter was still not with her, Mrs Yankinton calmed down a little. Now she was convinced that her daughter would be found in the end, slowly chewing on a hot ear of corn or scraping the bottom of a cup of ice-cream, taking a walk with one or two of her friends. Thus she calmed herself as the evening grew dark, and it was time for her to slice vegetables finely for a salad for supper. Mrs Yankinton got up from her seat and thanked 'the Polish couple', as she privately called my parents, especially when she needed to boost herself a bit, and turned to go. At the corner of Melchett and Mazeh streets, as she was walking towards Melchett, she suddenly saw her daughter in the company of two friends. The threesome were heading towards Yavneh— apparently they were walking Karni home, since they lived next door to each other—and their backs were towards Yehuda Halevi Street, as though they were returning from a place of danger, though this had not spoilt their mood and their pleasant chatter brought smiles to their faces. Mrs Yankinton, who caught all this with one sideways glance like a hunter waiting in ambush, first swelled with a feeling of great relief, but this soon gave way to a burst of disciplinary anger and an unexpected feeling of power that only great anger can stir up and maintain, however briefly, and she crossed Melchett Street diagonally and, running rapidly, almost barrelled into the threesome, separating them by planting a sudden slap on her daughter's cheek. The other two were frightened, but they told each other in their hearts, she is her mother, and so it is perfectly all right, while Karni burst into deafening sobs which ceased almost instantly because even then, as a small child, she had learnt to rein in her emotions in front of other people. And Mrs Yankinton dragged her daughter, half-running, or so it seemed to her husband watching from the window on Yavneh Street.

On other days, Karni arrived at my parents' home legally, after asking her parents and receiving their permission. Thus for example, a day after the incident of the slap, she came to us to play farm. On the white tile floor, eternally cold, I spread out the collection of farm animals which I had collected over the past few years. They included a donkey and a horse, a white dog with black spots posed to bark, a parrot, another horse and donkey, a pig, a cow, chickens, chicks and a duck. There was only one human being, a woman dressed in a knee-length blue skirt and white blouse. She wore a red kerchief and her right hand was extended to scatter some kind of grain which she had collected in her palms from the pouch she wore on a belt around her waist. The grain was meant for the farm animals, particularly the hens and chicks, for the woman was responsible for their health and wellbeing, and she ruled her farm. The farm animals were fashioned from one of the noble metals, painted in shiny colours. With the years, the paint had chipped in places, such as the spot where the woman's arm joined her elbow, or the duck's leg joint. The woman's nose was also flattened, as though she had suffered a blow or scrape which never healed. But this did not detract from her rustic beauty or her fresh complexion. We named the farm animals and gave them life stories and varied personalities. The chicks, however, held the lowest status. They ate seeds but were not distinguished by name or particular personalities. They were the masses. The farm also included a large house and a fence forming a spacious yard where, by early evening, all the animals congregated, and the fading daylight helped us trick them into finally lying down to sleep so they could rest a little. They, like us, were busy most of the day with intrigues and bids for power plotted in secret, as well as varied attacks of jealousy which led them to inform on each other and report names to the woman.

Karni had her own set of farm animals, very much like mine, but her collection expanded with the years, for Karni was an only child and her parents would deny her nothing that would make her happy. Essentially, the game was played similarly in both homes, except that the horse Lakik on Karni's farm did not bow his head in a motion of eating from the manger but always held it up, even rolling it back with a single joyful whinny as if he were a race horse instead of a farm horse and beast of burden. A labourer also worked on Karni's farm—a pioneer dressed in blue—and perhaps he was the husband or life partner of the woman from my farm. Other than that, a small red electric light burned on Karni's farm, illuminating the whole farm, the farmhouse and the brown fence surrounding it, and its light transported it far from Tel Aviv, from Karni's parents' house on Yavneh Street, until it became a radiant tableau, a strange treasure of beauty to be found only beyond a hidden, impenetrable barrier. I reflected that

I would never find myself among the animals of my friend's glowing farmstead and I would never experience the pleasure and tranquillity that radiated from the farmhouse and its fence. I knew this even then, as I watched how they were all led—the pioneer, the pigs, the guard dog, the chicks—perhaps not entirely at ease, under the tall legs of the Yankinton dresser which sheltered everything with a neat covering, medieval in character, like a well-defended and protecting castle, though it did so in the name of ordinary routine. But on the day after the slap, we played at my parents' house, and after the animals had been put to bed at the end of a long day, we turned to a game of swords which we swung at the lamp, calling 'Dulcinea, Love of my Life', jumping back and forth between the chairs and the couch, while the imaginary sword threatened the lamp hanging from the ceiling, which was also a windmill, and my father, who entered the room at that moment, bent his tall frame to avoid the sword's blow and swallowed a quiet smile, for he had also read Man of La Mancha as a child.

In those far-off days, I did not know that I was in the midst of something called childhood, which both penetrated me and surrounded me, and thus was found in everything around me. I could not know that, for I could not compare my childhood with other time periods which I had not experienced. I did know, however, that there were old people in the world, and also in Tel Aviv, even very many of them. My grandmother and grandfather were old, not like my parents who were not old but middle-aged. My friends openly competed among themselves over who had the youngest parents. Yael Hadar turned out to be the winner, with parents who were thirty-three, while my friend Karni was always the loser, for though her parents had not revealed the secret of their age, to the ordinary eye they looked almost old and even perhaps entirely old, at least to us. But Mr Yankinton, Karni's father, was an important man, and that compensated somewhat for the number of years of his life. In contrast, my parents, who were thirty-six at that time but looked younger than their age, were considered to be in the middle and did not arouse any particular attention, and that comforted me some-what. In children's picture books, old people were always depicted with bent backs and canes to help them walk. And when an elderly person sat on a chair or bench in a garden, his cane shook between his knees and his trembling fingers touched it lightly but did not rest on it. These were old people who were always in a good mood and they would direct advice towards us, the new generation. They did not suffer from diseases except for a certain difficulty in walking. In fact, they did not suffer at all and their only wish was to see their grandchildren's faces as much as possible and hear about their small successes. But in reality, and this I came to recognize only later, elderly people were not really like that. First of all, they were not always healthy. Sometimes they were ill, even with serious illnesses, and then they were no longer interested in their grandchildren. There were elderly people who even stopped recognizing their grandchildren when they got sick, as happened to my grandmother during her short final illness. She was struck by the iron knob on the window sash in her room when she bent down to pick up her wallet which had fallen, straightened up carelessly, and struck the window. Later I realized that the blow which struck my grandmother was a common and disastrous illness called a stroke, but my parents, like the rest of their extended family, were not in a hurry to expose their children too early to the troubles of human existence. A stroke was an incurable illness, thus it was negated by a cover story which fortified the premise that such things (like incurable illnesses) do not happen in good families. Hitting a window—maybe. But not a stroke. It became clear very quickly that the blow from the window had become fatal.

I went to visit my grandmother, who was lying in a spacious room, with another woman, in Assuta Hospital. I recognized my grandmother but she did not turn towards me, nor did she recognize me. Her eyes were as blue and watery as ever. Occasionally she muttered something in Polish. She dozed off for moments at a time. A nurse entered the room and turned to me: Who are you? Is this your grandmother? The nurse rolled back the blanket a bit and untied her hospital gown. —Do you see how smooth she is? she asked. What beautifully preserved skin she has, you wouldn't believe that she is so old. And after a moment's thought: We should only be like this when we get to her age.

Since the nurse's job was to care for the patients and I assumed that all her actions were proper and correct, and since she was paying compliments to my grand-mother, for of course it was good to have smooth, well-preserved skin in old age, I knew that I should welcome her words. But for some reason my heart was sad. I asked my mother for permission to return home alone and promised her I would be very careful to get on the right bus.

I knew that my grandmother was old and I did not like the nurse very much, but I did not know what old age was. In the same way, I did not know what youth was nor what childhood was. Everything I knew about old age came to me from outside. My grandmother's illness also came to me from outside, and the traces it left in me, which I will remember for ever, remain both understood and not understood, but this was not old age. I learnt about old age later, and in this way also learnt about childhood. But in those days, all I knew was that childhood was children's time of life and that some day it would end as though it had never been, when we would no longer be children, and only remember what we were like when we were children. Each of us would remember something else, and all of us collectively would remember all the impressions and experiences and heartbeats of childhood, and even so it would not be childhood that we would remember, for we cannot hold onto childhood within us except through continual forgetting. I, being a child, knew all this dimly, and even so I did not know childhood then. I wanted to reach the border where my childhood would end and be lost to me, but when I finally reached this border, I was momentarily distracted, and when I thought again about childhood, in the way that one always looks back one more time, I no longer saw it as it really was. What I saw was something that did not include childhood. I raised my arms and tried to stop the days passing like the pages of a calendar riffled by an unknown hand— like a skilled dealer shuffling cards in an old film—and I never said 'I found it.'

When my parents argued, I assumed that they fired insults at each other the way my friends and I insulted each other at certain times of the day. I shrank into an imaginary corner, covered my ears with my hands, and waited for the worst to pass as though it had never been. Only much later did I understand the character of adult arguments, which are more than anything a despairing cry of the incapacity to rejoice in being alive. When I finally understood this, my parents were no longer among the living. Also, I did not understand then the arguments of my uncle and aunt, my mother's younger brother and his wife, even though I witnessed them all too often. Every time I was invited to their home, when my parents dragged me to a family Shabbat visit, they were in the middle of an argument. Usually, my aunt would open the door for the guests sobbing: So, what do you say about this Carmi?

A year after they married, my aunt, my father's sister, brought us to the first flat of Carmi and his wife Lani in Jerusalem. At that time, my aunt lived in Jerusalem and worked as a saleslady in the bookshop of Old Steimatsky on Jaffa Road. My maternal uncle and aunt lived then on the ground floor of a large building, in a shady, tranquil neighbourhood. The two branches of the family thus became friends, and this friendship lasted for as long as they continued to live in the same city. After that, my maternal uncle and aunt moved to Tel Aviv and, when life's challenges became too demanding, the friendship came to an end. Therefore I accompanied my aunt, my father's sister Gina, to visit the young couple whose voices raised in argument were clearly audible as we moved from the well-groomed street into the stairwell. My Aunt Lani opened the door. —So, what do you say, Gina, about this der Carmi? she cried immediately. She called him der Carmi because of her German background and because she stood to inherit large sums of money, since Lev Roslin, the largest or perhaps even the only department store in Jerusalem, was founded and still owned by her great-grandfather, once the founder of the first department store chain in Berlin.

The flat door opened therefore to thunderous voices that poured out into the hallway. Lani complained, as far as I could understand, of her husband's lack of success in becoming rich. This was a complaint that would dog my uncle to the end of his adult life, finally causing his early death before his forty-sixth birthday. Suddenly she noticed our existence. —What beauties! she cried on seeing me and my sister, I remember when you came to our wedding! You had little black fur jackets and rosy cheeks! Do you remember that it snowed at our wedding? Wasn't it beautiful? Beautiful? Aunt Lani was exultant but she had not yet finished the argument with her husband. In fact, she was just announcing a brief time-out, after which the discussion picked up again with exactly the same words: Failure and more failure! Tell me, Gina, why don't we have even a small car? Why doesn't he bring money home? Look! We don't even have lightbulbs—as she held my aunt's hand and pulled her through a rapid tour of the flat— everything is falling from the ceiling, right? she turned to include me and my sister. Poor people's lamps! How is it that other people manage to buy cars? In this ugly argument, my uncle was actually being judged on his personality and not on his actions. The whole time my German aunt, as she was called in our house, was running around her spacious flat in the wealthy neighbourhood of Rehavia and complaining of her poverty. And yet there was a certain winning stupidity in her reasoning. I understood then that adults argue among themselves over money, and therefore money is a very bad thing or perhaps a very good thing. I asked my mother if our father was rich. —Rich? My mother laughed. —But does he have 100 pounds? I pursued and my mother said immediately: Yes, that he has. He has 100 pounds. I relaxed. If so, he is rich, I said. My mother did not contradict me. One hundred is a lot.

My aunt, my father's sister, would come to our house every Saturday night after Shabbat. She continued this custom even when she was married, but then it was still as though she came alone. Although sometimes she would bring her husband with her, dragged against his will, and from the moment he arrived he would sit down in the corner of the room on a chair which he placed at an angle, after he had collected a suitable pile of newspapers from all the rooms and strewn them haphazardly on the adjoining couch. And thus, with his yellow reading glasses sliding down to the edge of his bald forehead, plastering down his scant remaining hair, he would bury his head in the printed pages and not hear a thing. Yet he was really missing only on the evenings when he did not appear at all, when his slightly wide figure was entirely swallowed up and he did not stick out, even a little, beyond the margins of the open newspaper towards us. On those evenings my aunt would try to unburden herself to her siblings. Life alongside her husband was not comfortable or pleasant in the slightest, so it seemed, and with the help of the code name by which she referred to her husband outside of their home—'Little Idiot'—she told complex stories in which he played a decisive role, though not a flattering one. But when my father heard that another story was coming in which the name Little Idiot appeared, he would get up immediately, with a determined expression, and pronounce the sentence to which he would repair in such times of trouble: Ich vil nicht heiren! Meaning: I *do not want to hear*, and that was one of the only sentences in Yiddish whose meaning I understood immediately, for it was repeated many times in our house—in my father's eyes, the doings of a man and his wife were private, and invading them was no-one's business, even if we were expressly invited to do so by one of the married pair herself. But in my father's words I heard concern lest my aunt come to harm in the end, via such words, by shaking the stability of her marriage—she was married to a man who had divorced three wives before her, without children, and her marriage was referred to as a 'late marriage'. If she remained alone, who would look after her? In fact, my aunt was worried too. My father and my aunt were all that was left for each other after the great war in which the rest of their family had been systematically slaughtered. My aunt was quite theatrical and given to exaggeration. But in this matter it would have been difficult to exaggerate. Sometimes she suffered terrible panic attacks, when she would call our house to make sure that nothing awful had happened since she had left a few hours earlier. More than once I was the one who answered the telephone. My aunt, on the verge of tears, would ask me where my father was. If he was not at home at that moment she would ask: Are you sure? And also: Where is he exactly? You're not hiding anything? I was afraid that she would get up and go to every place I mentioned, and yet I wanted to bring her a bit of peace of mind, so I remained silent. I did not know what to say. And in doing so I knew that if I were in distress as she was now, my aunt would never withhold information from me on my father's whereabouts, if she were to possess such information, since she was, as I already understood as a child, a speaker of truth and a better person than I. My aunt, my father's sister, would not ask herself, for example, what Mr Potorek, director of the elegant women's fashion salon located on the second floor of a roofed building on Allenby Street, would say if my father were really there at that moment, and in this salon they spoke only Polish and stepped on soft rugs with delicate shoes (Mr Potorek was my father's most prestigious client and bought wares from him twice a year—it was his name which enabled my father to market all the rolls of fabric which kept his textile factory in business), when he would suddenly see a short woman with unruly hair, not like that of the Polish women who made sure to visit the hairdresser once a week, and a face tormented with trouble, who would arrive at his salon on the second floor and fall with a sigh of relief onto my father's shoulder, for she did not reach his neck, and tears would pour down her face as though she had found her lost child.

My aunt, as far as I could guess, would not have brought up such doubts. She would have given me whatever information she had on my father's whereabouts at any given moment, if I had asked about him. In the same way, she would not have wondered whether her action might cause harm, even indirectly, to my father's business dealings or his reputation. Such questions would not occur to her at all. But I asked myself all these questions and thus, even if I did not know exactly where my father was at that moment, I did not say anything because of those doubts which were always at the back of my mind, even if they never occurred to my aunt.

Many years have passed since then. Mr Potorek's elegant salon with its two front halls for his guests who landed there by chance from the bustle of the street, and the inner hall dedicated to women of quality, each one well connected because of her money or her husband's high position, for whom a special appointment was made, at a specific date and time, for an interview or a fitting, with Mr Potorek himself serving her—gone for ever. For my uncle, though his wife mocked him for an ingrained inability to advance in life like other people, her derision did not diminish his good will and his joy in existence for as long as he lived in Jerusalem, and he would sell his rolls of merchandise in a small wholesale shop on Shammai Street, and he himself would speak with his Arab customers in their tongue, which he had picked up just by hearing it, just as earlier he had spoken with English customers in their tongue, which he had picked up in the same way, moved to Tel Aviv and there lost all his regular customers, while no new customers came to the shopfront he rented next to the Romano Building. This uncle has since passed away, but the mocking cries meant to spur him to greater achievements did not cease until two days before his death, when his wife suddenly realized that this time the situation was really serious, and that my uncle would never stand on his feet again and run to the shop. My uncle's two shops, the one on Shammai Street and the new one, next to the Romano Building in Tel Aviv, disappeared without a trace, along with my uncle's life. Mr and Mrs Yankinton are also no longer alive, nor are Yael Hadar's young parents, and my aunt, my father's sister, disappeared one day in the corridors of Balfour Hospital in Tel Aviv, and my father's shadow on the wall, whenever he used to enter the half-darkened room where we lay before sleep, my sister and I, in two adjacent beds and discussed everything that had occupied us during the day—we chattered ceaselessly until my father entered, expecting that we would not want to utter our secrets in his hearing and thus we would finally go to sleep, and this shadow, which angered me at first, but won in the end, so that we fell asleep from weariness—it too has disappeared, just like my father's motion of bowing his head and shoulders, which he had adopted to protect himself from the blows of the imaginary sword which I held as I jumped with my friend Karni on my parents' dilapidated couch and shouted Dulcinea! Only my aunt's feeling of terror has not disappeared. It was passed on to me, where it grew stronger and more rooted. It is unwanted, unnecessary, breeds resentment in anyone who does not carry it like me, distances strangers from me, and like a termite, to whose presence one gradually becomes accustomed, so that its faint gnawing ultimately brings him a certain peace, reassuring him that everything is as usual and everything is good, and thus he manages to fall asleep while the worm is still munching away, first his desk chair and then the table and the coffee table, and finally the bed on which he is sleeping, so I befriended the worm and became subservient to it, and only in the moments when it falls asleep exhausted do I remember all this.

Sometimes my parents would go out to watch a film. From time to time they felt compelled to add a measure of optimism to the secular side of their lives, and expressed this sense with the words, 'Let's go to the cinema,' which was uttered as half-question, half-statement. They usually preferred the Ophir Theatre over all others, perhaps because of its proximity to our house. But sometimes they went to Sderot or as far as the Esther Cinema. They never once visited the new cinemas built in the north of the city, such as the Tehelet Theatre or the North Theatre. When my parents went out, our flat instantly changed its demeanour. My sister and I fixed ourselves supper and then served it to ourselves. There was no sound except our voices and the clatter of dishes and utensils. We spread out a small tablecloth—folding it so that it would cover only half the table—on the high table in the living room, usually covered with a sheet of thick glass held in place by four pieces of pink rubber—the sort of rubber stoppers, time-worn, which had almost entirely lost their once-proud round shape, and the thick glass continued to sink onto them and also on my forearms when I did my homework, only starting at nightfall, as I did every day, even when guests came to visit my parents, and I, bent over books and notebooks from various subjects at an hour approaching midnight, caused them amazement mixed with pity—on this table we now spread out the folded tablecloth. My sister cut up vegetables to take the place of a prepared salad: cucumbers, tomatoes, slices of radish. Those were the vegetables which always appeared on our table at suppertime—in those days, the local shops did not yet sell red bell peppers—and then she addressed herself to making a two-egg omelette. When the omelette was heated in the frying pan, my sister added a few slices of tomato which she had set aside for that purpose, and sprinkled a little salt. She stirred the mixture with a spoon and fork as it heated. My aunt, my father's sister, had taught us this style of preparing an omelette, which she called 'Spanish style', and therefore one could not assume that it would be acceptable to my mother or that this type of omelette would appear on our table regularly, not even occasionally for variety. My mother was conservative and never felt the need to accept suggestions for change, particularly not from my aunt. And now, while my parents were out at the cinema, we did the simple and obvious thing in such cases and made a Spanish omelette. Our parents had not yet returned when we got undressed and ready for bed, and not even when we got under the light summer blankets and wrapped ourselves in them like an embrace. On that late evening before sleep, we did not talk much between ourselves. Now, when we could talk as much as we wanted with no one to bother us, there was nothing to talk about. The day's experiences faded away. My sister drowsed off. —Are you asleep? I asked her. I remained alone. I went to the window. From the fourth floor, the street looked long, with nothing in sight at its end. I knew that my parents were supposed to return, and would return. But this knowledge was not certain. Over my bed by the window, the night breeze flowed into the room. A moth that had found its way into the flat beat its wings against the walls. It cannot find its way in the dark, I reflected. Its face, like a corpse's skull, disturbed my rest. Now I was already frightened, at only 10 p.m., and only near 11 did I hear the sound of feet scraping the outer steps of the building, accompanied by fragments of quiet speech, and then the rattle of the key in the lock. When they came into the flat, my parents continued speaking quietly. —So as not to wake the girls, they said. —I see they prepared themselves a big supper, said my father, meaning the few leftovers remaining on the kitchen counter, and he shook out the tablecloth, still on the table, into the wastebasket. —Yes, said my mother, eyeing the small frying pan, slightly burnt, containing the remains of an egg and fried tomato which my sister had forgotten to clean. —That's strange, my mother said. At that moment I came out to them. In fact, I ran. —Why so late? I started to complain, but all my distress disappeared and was forgotten in the full presence of my parents in our little kitchen, and thus other questions came to me: How was the film, did you have fun? Was it funny or sad? What was it called? Who were the actors? My parents did not know how to answer all my questions. To answer the last question required a certain knowledge and even expertise in film. And my parents did not demonstrate skills in anything which society respected in those days.

My friends all collected cards which bore the faces of actors or actresses who appeared primarily in Hollywood films, and sometimes they showed the upper part of their bodies as well. I also had a nice collection of such cards, which we called 'Artistes'. Artistes were purchased at newsstands along the avenues of the city, as well as at stationery shops. I heard then that at the Da'at-Sderot Library, called thus because of its proximity to the Sderot Theatre, they were giving out free Artistes to readers who exchanged more than one book a week. Up to now, my primary means of expanding my collection had been to trade Artistes with my friends. For two Bette Davis, who was considered ugly, one could get one Betty Grable. For Paul Robeson, whom we considered to be a movie actor, we got Shirley Temple, and if one could hold out in the negotiations—a Betty Grable as a bonus. It was difficult to increase one's collection significantly through trading alone. What is more, the rules of trading were unclear, and changed with each neighbourhood or street on which the collectors lived, and like always, the results of the negotiations tended to favour the less-interested customers who did not even show any eagerness and were generally the wealthy girls who had big rooms filled with new toys. These girls did not have any urgent need to trade, for their parents would buy them new Artistes in shops whenever they wanted, but they enjoyed wielding their power and traded with us over and over, always coming away with a significant profit. As a result of these trades, my collection shrunk while their collection, which was already large, did not lose anything, and even increased in size. Thus, when I heard of the Da'at-Sderot Library's generous offer, there was nothing to do but move to that library from the one we currently used, and I did so, though not without a certain hesitation. Thus I switched to the Da'at Library next to the Sderot Theatre. Only years later did I understand that the prizes which the library offered for rapid reading were actually a brilliant marketing move which was years ahead of its time, and it seemed that the Da'at-Sderot Library also intended thus to increase the clientele of the adjacent cinema, which screened primarily Hollywood films, mostly those in which the actual figures of our Artistes played a significant part, so that the faithful and hardworking readers increased their collections of Artistes while expanding the profits of both the library and the adjacent cinema, for from then on they did not miss a single film in which one of their Artistes played, and they also read more books, so this was one of the rare instances where all partners in a deal came out equally satisfied.

But not everything went so smoothly nor suited all the participants' wishes. Sometimes, a child showed up at the library who refused to accept the prize card he was given, claiming that this card was not 'worth it'— Sonja Haney, for example, who was just an ice-skater, and in addition, 'I already have her in my collection.' The librarian did not usually accept such claims, and would insist on giving the child specifically the Sonja Haney card, telling him that it is always possible that he is not accurately describing reality, and that even an additional Sonja Haney card is useful, since it can be traded. Though it was true that more than once a child would colour the truth, and especially when the card offered him was one of the dubious Artistes, he would defend his stand passionately against the librarian and pretended to be insulted. But the child's right of appeal was only rarely honoured, and in these cases the librarian was always the sole judge. Even when the child waved before the librarian two worn Sonja Haney cards from the collection which he always carried in his pocket, declaring the words, 'I already have two of them!', the librarian most often dismissed this proof with an expression of complete indifference which said: The Da'at-Sderot Library is not required to respond. In such a case, the child remained frustrated, filled with a sudden inchoate feeling that he had never before encountered, which said: A clear injustice has been done to me and I cannot do anything about it because the bureaucracy, the government, the powers that be, all are immeasurably stronger than me, and they are all before me now in the guise of the librarian.

I switched to Da'at-Sderot from the Izeresky Library. This was a large library which had been built opposite the Ophir Theatre. It contained a large, long hall, with all four walls lined with books from floor to ceiling. At the end of the room, a ladder led up to the second floor, called the 'gallery', and from the top of the ladder one had to open a small trapdoor in the ceiling and insert one's head, while struggling slightly with the cover—which was on one side the ceiling of the library hall, and on the other side the floor of a small living space—by butting it with one's head, in order to slip into the gallery itself. The extended Izeresky family—father, mother, adult daughter and grand-mother—would do this regularly for, as I only found out years later, they lived there on the second floor of the library, and each time any family member wanted to go home, he had to climb the ladder and push up the cover by holding his head correctly but not comfortably, and thus pass into the family's modest living quarters. There was no other door.

The Izeresky family had been somehow uprooted from Stalin's Soviet Union, for unclear reasons, and they brought with them the first stock of books, to which more were added in the following years, as Mr Izeresky bought them from libraries which had been dismantled and whose owners were trying to recover something from their investment by selling the books they no longer needed. With time it became clear to me that most of the books filling the shelves of Mr Izeresky's library, from the floor to the ceiling, were written in Russian and were intended to meet the demands of the Russian speakers among us, and only a minority of the shelves carried books written in Hebrew. I insisted—

though not immediately—that Mr Izeresky himself, a redhead with a fiery red, bushy beard, give us books translated from Russian which praised the Soviet revolution while hiding chapters of its history. Thus, for example, I received again and again—Mr Izeresky was never satisfied with a first reading, as he called it, first and therefore not effective, and would push on us the 'recommended books' endlessly—Panfilov's *Men*, from whom I learnt of the wonderful methods in the great revolution in education, and Gorky's *Mother* and Michael Strogoff and his marvellous acts of heroism for which he was ultimately compensated in a marvellous way, and *Siberia, Land of Miracles*—the script. I read all these until I was sick of the Russian Revolution and its achievements. I did not entirely understand then, however, that it was impatience with these books that ate at me, and I only knew that it would be hard for me to withstand the magic that the Da'at Library's offer had opened before me. At the same time, in those days I finished reading the entire collection of books translated from Russian that were in the Izeresky Library—beyond those, there were no more books written in Hebrew or translated into Hebrew—and Mr Izeresky himself would not leave the selection of books up to his readers but would force them to accept the choices he made for them, and here the child's muttered protest 'I already read that' would not help, for Mr Izeresky would recoil with an expression such as: 'What do you mean, read? You read it the first time! A reading which is worth nothing!' and would add 'Good for nothing!' an insult which he heard once from one of the red-faced old immigrants from Czarist Russia. In such instances, I felt that the time was fast approaching when Mr Izeresky would kick me out of the library too, reprimanding me for ingratitude. Indeed, in those days   I wanted more than anything to switch to the Da'at-Sderot Library, yet in a way that would not raise Mr Izeresky's ire. My good parents permitted me this one time to speak an untruth, and when I arrived at the Izeresky library, carrying Panfilov's *Men* after the third reading, I muttered something to the effect that my parents would no longer allow me to take books out of the library because 'reading books was a waste of time in their opinion'. Mr Izeresky jumped up from his seat: Don't let you read?! What are you saying? Such bourgeois!—Miserable bourgeois, he continued muttering to himself as he drew a thick red line across my reader's card, and thus I left the Izeresky Library and moved over to the Da'at Library next to the Sderot Theatre.

Da'at was a moderate-sized library whose chief advantage was its selection of Artistes. As to its books, I had read most of them in the shelter of other libraries. I waited patiently in line to get A *Tree Grows in Brooklyn*, whose Hebrew translation had been published that year. Other than that, there were few advantages to the Da'at Library. In the meantime, my fascination with collecting Artistes gave way to new fads such as collecting 'goldies' or drying flowers in an album. During that period, we all collected shiny pictures of angels whose lower bodies were sunk in clouds, thereby obviating the need to decide whether they were fundamentally male or female, or if they belonged to either sex at all, or whether they were telling us, wrapped in a thin loin-cloth, that we should not be so occupied with definitions and that not everything is exact in our world. These angels had rosy cheeks, and when we scrutinized them long enough, we could observe that they actually had the faces of babies, and perhaps they themselves were fully formed infants who had not yet been born. Though peeling at the edges, these pictures were of impressive size and we called them prizes—a name with the very best connotations—and they comforted us for our drab existence in the world. One way or another, the glow of the old film stars faded away to nothing, and there was no longer anything to draw me to the Da'at Library.

When I left the Da'at Library, I had already read most of the books—novels, novellas, travelogues and adventure stories—that made the rounds of the city's libraries at that time. But there was one more library that I decided to try. To myself, I called it 'the Round One' because it shared the facade of the round building of Nachmani Street, looking towards the central square of Little Tel Aviv, with a large pay laundry which was one of the first generation of such services, and the library somehow complemented it. The laundry occupied most of the round building's facade, and included a large, steamy hall where the temperatures reached 40 degrees Celsius. Each client was required to bring his dirty laundry wrapped in one of his bedsheets and tied with a granny knot at the four corners of the sheet. Thus, the sheet served simultaneously as an item to be washed and a container to hold the entire load of laundry. The client would turn over his laundry to the machine boy without a word, for the racket was intolerable. Even if he wanted to say something, he would have to yell, and no one would have heard him or even tried to hear what he was saying. Even so, many people milled about because each of them, after turning over his bundle of laundry to the machine boy, was filled with an inchoate fear that his laundry would never return to him, or at best would get mixed in with someone else's (of a family with many children, including soiled babies or perhaps a cynical old man who changed his clothes and bedding once in a great while and sent them to the laundry only when he had no choice left. If this happens, the client would think to himself, who will I turn to and who will listen to me if no one hears anything here anyway except the clatter of the machines? And the machine boy seemed to him like a low-ranking clerk from Hell whose only job was to make sure that the system functioned properly.) Thus the customers wandered restlessly among the machines, with gravely worried expressions, and the odour of bleach vaguely irritated their nervous systems. And while they were expecting the worst to happen to their possessions, I slipped into the small library, the Round Library, as I called it, which had been established next to the laundry in a modest shopfront, almost unnoticed by passers-by. The dull pounding of the washing machines reverberated there throughout the day, any time the adjacent laundry was operating, washing over its walls with a kind of serenity, for it was like the rush of distant waves. The library looked brand new, but all its books were old and exuded a smell of age. The librarian was a pleasant man of thirty or thirty-five, or so it seemed to me then, with black hair pulled back and a black yarmulke placed on top. I was happy that the librarian's yarmulke was black and not crocheted with an indeterminate colour. I thought to myself, how good it would be to marry that librarian and sit with him behind the counter, waiting for readers to come. And if a client entered the library, I would jump up right away and lead him to his favourite shelf so that he could choose whatever book he wished. And I would speak gently to my husband and he would place his arm around my shoulders and ask: Could I offer my lady a cup of tea or coffee with milk? We received some wonderful coffee today, a gift from one of the readers. Thus I imagined my life whenever I entered the library. But the librarian with the yarmulke barely noticed me, even though he climbed on a stepstool to offer me *Nobody's Boy* by Hector Malot and I cried buckets while reading it because every page brought new losses to the family members who were perishing one by one. But when I returned the book, he did not ask: Did you like this book? Did you understand everything written in it? Nor did I think about the librarian as long as I was busy reading books. I only thought about him when I came to the library. The Round Library was my last library before I signed up for the real last library—Mira, named after the wife of the chief librarian, who thus strove to express his love for her. After Mira Library, which was established on the edge of the square named for Tzina Dizengoff, wife of an early mayor, whose name sounded so strange to our ears, but surely she also was loved in her own way by her husband, I did not exchange any more books in a public library. Instead, books came to me as though of their own accord, or at least in ways that were sometimes strange. Though I often bought them in shops, and sometimes in second-hand shops, and always spent more on their purchase than was allowed or possible, the period of libraries in my life had come to an end.

Looking back again, I remembered Apelrud. I only remembered him in retrospect, as though he had just come to me now from the outside, for Apelrud, the sole owner of the Apelrud Library on Allenby Street, acted as though he was our master. We hated him and feared him. But Apelrud did not know how to forgive us for that. He demanded of his young readers that they recount, precisely and clearly, the contents of the book they had read at home and were now trying to return to the library. If the recounting did not seem fluent or precise enough—as almost always happened—he would burst out laughing, pronounce the reader stupid and send him home again to reread the book. Thus the library's stock of books remained almost static and was almost never offered for circulation, as is usually done in libraries, and what is more, the rules of the library, which Mr Apelrud himself had laid down, forbade readers, even if they passed the tests, to exchange more than one book a week, while the readers who failed remained humiliated, to the tyrant's joy, and were sent home hugging the old book to themselves, hoping that their mother or sister did not greet them with the question: 'Which book did you take out now?' This whole scene unfolded before my eyes only later, while for almost all of my early childhood I simply feared Mr Apelrud and worried that I would not meet his demands, and thus part of my pleasure in reading had already been stolen from me even then. In its wake, other things were also taken from me. Taken, but not stolen, as Mr Apelrud stole my pleasure in reading and my natural confidence in my ability to read, understand and remember. Indeed, I had managed to read very few books in the Apelrud period when I suddenly fell ill and became bedridden.

I fell ill with scarlet fever. My case was declared serious and my sister was removed from the house so that she would not catch my illness. Our favourite doctor, who lived on the first floor and always ended his visits with memories and lessons from the war days, moved about the flat with a grim face, scolding my mother for not adequately airing the sickroom. Once, after she closed the bathroom door too forcefully, he shouted: Where were you born? Where did you come from? They changed my bedsheets every day, and at those times I had to leave my place and move from the bed to the large chair. My mother supported me as I walked but the room receded before me. In those days I could read as much as I wanted. From my parents I received *101 Stories*, a book which I had long craved, voluminous and bound in green velvet. Then I received *From Dan to Beersheba* in two volumes, which I desired from the first time I saw it on Karni's bookshelf. There I learnt about the troubles of the first pioneers who settled among the swamps of Hadera and were killed off by the Anopheles mosquitos. Out of pity and admiration for the pioneers, I decided then to be a member of a kibbutz when I grew up. For being a kibbutz member and being a pioneer seemed to me one and the same thing, or at least extremely similar one to the other. But if an Anopheles mosquito came near me, I continued to plan my future, I would spray it with Flit. Thus I decided, and wondered why the pioneers had not done so. A little Flit would have changed their lives and left most of them still alive. Would they have lived until today, or perhaps their way of life had sucked out all their strength and they would have died young anyway? My father went to Apelrud Library instead of me, and returned bearing two books. Indeed, my father was not obliged to recount the book which he returned in my name to Mr Apelrud himself, whom several of my friends had nicknamed 'Red', since two of them, whose opinion was respected by all the rest, claimed that they saw something red peeping out from the librarian's trsouer leg when he climbed on the ladder to reach a book on a high shelf. Indeed, Mr Apelrud always wore very skimpy shorts, summer and winter, and anyway no one would cast doubt on the two friends' reports, and my father, who did not know of the nickname Red when he went to Apelrud Library instead of me, returned with two books and Mr Apelrud's promise that for as long as I was ill, I could exchange as many books as I wanted, even one every day. Since then, many years have passed. I have known people who have attained marvellous achievements and received monetary and honorary prizes, accompanied by detailed explanations diligently written by the secretaries of committees created in their honour. But even in their light, my father's achievement does not pale as I think of his image, carrying two books which he had rescued for me from the underworld.

But in the following days, when my fever rose and did not fall again, unlike the previous days when it had risen and fallen alternately, I did not look at my father's face, nor did I ask after my sister whom I had not seen for many days, so that I had almost forgotten what she looked like. The flat was perpetually shrouded in darkness. The slightest ray of light hurt my eyes. At night, my parents lit a small lamp in the adjacent room but even that, when it reached me indirectly through the large glass door, caused me pain. I wanted to say, Turn off the light! but my throat thickened to a heavy lump of distress and I did not speak. Dimly I saw my mother and father sitting by my bedside. I would fall asleep for a few moments and when I awoke, they would be still sitting there in the same position, and so it was all that night and the next day. In the evening, the doctor arrived bearing a prescription for a new medicine. My father hurriedly donned his outer garments and left the house. The medicine was sold only in one pharmacy, belonging to an Arab in Jaffa. When my father returned, everything seemed to me all jumbled together: the bottle of medicine, my mother's face, the Arab from Jaffa standing behind the medicine counter, the doctor, my father wrapped in his outdoor garments, my faraway sister, they all held their breath for a moment and I breathed. Was I saved? Sometimes, for a brief moment, after all the many days that have passed since that day and night when my father and mother sat motionless by my bed, I remember them. Now I am in their debt and they are not in mine. But how does one repay debts to those who have died? They return to me in my memory, still sitting, the light from the adjacent room blurring their images and hurting my eyes. They told me that everything is open now, not just for me but for everyone, and Death is generous, so they said. —But then you wanted Life so much, I protested in a whisper. —Yes, they said. And how I loved them then.

My initial recovery was rapid and easy. But I returned to full health only slowly, and even then something of the illness remained in me, just as there was something healthy in me even in the midst of my illness. The illness needed health because without it, it would be death and not illness, just as health needed illness, even a tiny fraction of it, in order to exist in a world where nothing is perfect. Yet, as the days passed, life returned and donned the routine which had guided it in the past. My parents once again began to receive guests at home and to go out in the evenings. But in that period I had already told myself that all my old fears and worries were no more than false delusions, and the remnant of the illness in me said that only now would I know how to worry properly and for real. I became addicted to my fears. I forced myself to drink black coffee, strong and bitter, which I prepared for myself the moment I heard my parents' footfalls fading away down the stairs, and I was determined to stay awake, awaiting their return, if they would return, I said to myself, for this would be my rule from now on, no longer to expect time to unfold properly, time, which pretends to adapt itself to our hopes.

But this time my parents did not go out to the cinema. They did not savour the fears of Barbara Stanwyck, the wealthy quadriplegic who accidently discovers that her husband is planning her death before daybreak. This time they themselves were caught in a web of deceit by someone with no conscience. My father, despite bitter experience, had not lost his fundamental faith in human promises and agreements—he discovered that a sum of money, which he had placed in the hands of someone presenting himself as an expert in installing electric boilers, had disappeared with the man himself, and the promise that soon we would all be able to bathe in unlimited hot water, meaning hot water flowing from the taps, faded away before our eyes.

On that evening, my parents left on a desperate journey with very little chance of success—in fact, almost no chance at all. Since my father had paid up front the entire sum he owed for the electric boiler and its installation, a boiler which he had never seen and, as time went by, the chances of ever seeing it became less and less, he understood that he had been cheated. Understood but still did not accept it. My parents assumed that if they could only manage to lay eyes again on the man who cheated them, they would also manage to persuade him to return their money. My father had an address which the man had given him. My parents did not ask themselves why someone whose intention was to cheat innocent people would give them his real address. On the folded note that remained in my father's possession, two lines were written: Avrahami, Shikun Vatikim 4, Netanya. To get there, they first boarded a bus which took them from Allenby to the Tel Aviv Central Bus Station. There they asked, at the small information counter built next to the pavement leading to the men's toilets, where one had to stoop in just the right way to hear the clerk's words, about buses to Netanya. The next bus left at 2.50. Thus, without noticing, my parents had already spent two whole hours travelling. They arrived at the Netanya Central Bus Station after another hour, and then took an internal bus in order to reach the Shikun Vatikim. At Shikun Vatikim 4, there was no family by the name of Avrahami. They searched fruitlessly along both sides of the building and in the back but did not find a second entrance. Someone said that there was also a Shikun Vatikim in Dora, an old neighbourhood next to Netanya. The bus to Dora arrived only four times a day. Evening was approaching as they boarded the second to last bus to Dora. In Dora, a neighbourhood populated primarily by poor immigrants, my parents already began to widen their efforts. First they had to find any Shikun Vatikim at all, but one could not be found. —There was one once but it closed, said a young man pushing a cart of corn, all the old people died. That was a joke. At that point, my parents were close to collapsing. They had to choose: run and perhaps catch the last bus to Netanya, or stay here and spend the night between two large chicken coops in a farmer's yard, with a soft plume of duck and chicken feathers to cushion their bed. My parents decided to be law-abiding, and boarded the last bus leaving Dora for an unknown direction. When they arrived home after midnight, they were silent. Not like times when they came home from the cinema in a good mood. I climbed under the blanket and shut my eyes. I understood that something bad had happened, something bad to the family. Indeed, it was three years before my father paid out money a second time to purchase the boiler that would heat our water. In the meantime, the condition of boilers worldwide, and in Israel, had improved slightly. A matte chrome finish was added which promised to maintain the heat of the water better, reducing the amount of electricity wasted. This time my father turned to a large company which was expert in producing newspaper advertisements promising good things, and when the boiler arrived at our house as promised, a special person (an engineer) was sent to accompany it and explain to us how to use it. We no longer mentioned the first boiler. It was as though the second boiler had come to repair the inadequacies of the boiler which did not exist. But there was an illusion in this. The lack of the first boiler, which was its main fault, was not erased. It continued to dog us because it took hold, as all lacks do, in things which surrounded our life and thus created for us a comfortable and stable environment, as they penetrated and seeped into us, until the day when it would take control of all these, in the name of its only master, the void. Indeed, when someone mentioned the name Netanya in my parents' presence, I saw a shadow cross their faces. But no one ever mentioned the name Dora to them, since it was a backwater neighbourhood whose main road was covered in mud each winter, it had almost no pavements, and its residents were few and poor. But Dora lodged itself in my memory from then on because it was there that my parents understood that they would never again succeed in their lives, even though the word 'success' was not really comprehensible to them, and they had received its meaning only from other people, and from newspapers and radio broadcasts. This success would never fall to them. They understood this, and in Dora they also made peace with the thought, which in some way was passed on to me as well, and I lived it and afterwards passed it on to my own children.

But on the day when these things took place, I did not yet know this. On that day, in maths class, the teacher handed back the exam for the second trimester, on which both I and my deskmate Karni received the grade 'insufficient', a term invented once upon a time by a well-intentioned teacher who wished to reduce the suffering of those who failed. It was subsequently approved by the pedagogical council of those long-ago days (indeed, from that council, only that single word remains and no more. The council was a shadowy entity which I struggled unsuccessfully to picture in my mind, for, throughout my school years, every report card bore a stamp in pale blue letters, 'By the decision of the Pedagogical Council'. I wondered if this organization would be able to distinguish between one pupil and another on the day it took command, with human fate in its hands, whether it would know whom to take pity on, whom to abandon to his fate?) At first glance, these words appeared somewhat encouraging: the child did not make enough effort, they said; he did not try hard enough up to now, tomorrow is still ahead of us. In the end, however, that brought us scant comfort. Perhaps that was enough for the generations who came before us, who could encourage themselves by their own force of will, but they did not need words as we did, and per-haps the words themselves had lost their power and become bare, shrivelled, dressed in wrinkled summer dresses which had been stored all winter by mistake under heavy blankets and now were taken thoughtlessly from the closet and placed on a naked body, barbed, 'insufficient'. A bite by a dog who then disappeared. A bite which could not be healed. If in fact the dog was infected, it was your job to prove it. The onus was on you, but the wound bled and foretold bad things to come. Thus I sat on the high kitchen chair next to my parents' bedroom. The winter sun had not yet warmed the furniture and household objects but spread a powdery white coat of light over everything. And from my perch on the chair, the floor was very far away. I cried not only over my failure but also over my stupidity—when I had finished answering all the questions, which included many division problems, I had glanced at Karni's answer sheet which she had placed before her, finished and ready to be collected by the test monitor. All her answers had been different from mine, and I had concluded that all her answers, unlike mine, were correct. Therefore I had erased all my answers and, in bold pencil, written Karni's answers instead. The good Karni had even angled her page towards me so that I could copy from it more easily without anyone seeing. In doing so, I had ignored the fact, which I discovered only in the coming years, that the laws of mathematics do not tolerate arbitrary answers, even if they are the most correct in the world, without an explanation of how one arrived at the answer, and without this they are worthless. I had so burnt to save myself by correcting my answers according to the fleeting model which my friend had offered me, that I had not stopped to ask myself whether my answers might have been correct from the beginning, unlike the answers I was now copying at no small risk to myself. Such a possibility had not occurred to me then, or even now as I sat on the chair, but events finally proved it to be in fact true, and meanwhile, out of all the children in the class, only Karni and I received the grade 'insufficient', and now I sat on the high chair in my parents' house and cried, more from regret than from pain over the miserable grade. And indeed, from then on the low grade faded from my life as though it had never been, but the regret has stayed with me. I never take an action without later considering it with regret. I never make a choice without finding it the next day to be somehow mistaken, as if in a kind of momentary flight which convulses my heart as it passes over me. How many words remained unsaid, how many celebrations were tainted with alienation and moments of coldness, how many understandings hid a lack of desire to understand. What good was regret in all these instances, when it could not repair anything? I perched myself on the chair and cried and my parents comforted me without knowing the reason. And when I told them that I had received 'insufficient' in maths, they said: That's all? That's nothing.

After the affair of the electric boiler, my parents slowly recovered their strength. Their faces had undergone a change when they returned from Dora, a change which was visible for some weeks before it finally faded away. On the outside, everything remained as it had been before. Only on the outside, for time never ceases to alter us and itself, and when it does so with mercy we may not feel it, as long as no major event forces us to look again at what we saw yesterday, when we told ourselves that nothing had changed, and suddenly it has become unrecognizable. Then we pay for the long periods of calm with a new sorrow.

But even the affair of the 'insufficient' in maths weakened its hold on my soul. I learnt a practical lesson; on future maths tests, I no longer copied anything from my friend's answer page. In fact, on all future tests, I would never again experience that powerful urge to copy from my neighbour's notebook, but this did not make me feel more satisfied with myself or more sure of my actions, for the need which impelled me then to the act of copying did not disappear with that single failure, or, as people say, the lesson of life.

At the next parents' meeting, which my parents attended together as they always did, hoping thus to conquer the boredom of waiting for long hours outside rooms with closed green doors, sitting cramped on chairs meant for young pupils, the homeroom teacher scanned the list of pupils' names in the class roster before she lifted her head to look at them. A few minutes passed in which the teacher strained to remember, while my parents quaked a little. —She's as quiet as a dove, the teacher finally said, I don't even remember exactly what she looks like. But my mother did not give up. —And how are her grades? she asked. —Her grades are OK, no complaints. The teacher snapped the book closed to signify that the short meeting was finished. My parents rose from the small chairs. When they came home, I saw them from a distance, coming up the faraway street, becoming larger and clearer to my eyes with every passing moment, and yet they were supporting each other as they walked. Suddenly they looked tired to me, enrobed in advanced age, even though at that time they were no more than forty. I worried that they would not have the strength to climb the twenty stairs at the entrance to the street, which had no railing, and then the forty more stairs inside the building. Perhaps because of this, and because of tense uncertainty about my academic achievement, I felt my heart pounding wildly and invisible blood vessels throbbing in my throat. But then the sound of the key turning in the lock filled the flat, and my parents were home again. —What did the teacher say? —He said you are as quiet as a dove, my father said, hiding the rest from me. After that he pronounced the same phrase a few more times, quiet as a dove, a phrase which had no empirical basis, since doves actually utter loud cries of mourning. And I thought about this until I fell asleep.

Every evening at about 11, Mrs Yankinton prepared herself (it was important to keep up a modest but pleasant front, and absolutely never negligent, thus she also needed to run a comb through her hair) to report to her place by the radio, and after that by her television set, while the government channel made its own preparations to broadcast the national anthem and thus close the day's programming. The anthem was played without words but accompanied by appropriate drums, and afterwards, close to the end, the trumpets joined in. In the days of television, these were joined by a picture of an Israeli flag, new, with perfect, clean edges, waving in a strong wind, which was not like the real world, in which flags which wave in the wind collect stains and dirt and absorb clouds of dust after only a quarter hour of waving, and thus lose their initial festive look. But the flags on television were always new and they even split into three smaller flags every time, towards the end of the national anthem, when the trumpets came in.

Mrs Yankinton would stand the whole time at tense attention, struggling to hold back the tears, for she felt that if not, she would burst into uncontrollable sobs. And despite the fact that these would be tears of joy and emotion, she did not want to worry the members of her family. But the rest of the Yankinton family—consisting of no more than a father and his daughter accepted the mother's ways and forgave her for them, mostly because they did not see them as particularly strange, for a great affection for the anthem and national flag was not foreign to them, and in the end, it was not so long ago, as she would often recount when she was out in society, that she would line Karni's baby carriage with live grenades and the most lethal sort of dumdum bullets, against the laws of maternal nature, and thus, without arousing the suspicion of the authorities, supported our fighters in Jaffa and other places, members of the Etzel underground movement. For all this, the infant Karni served as an unwitting courier, and Mrs Yankinton—Mother Courage, mother of wars. But now, what was left of all that? To stand rigidly at attention facing the dials of the radio receiver after hearing the broadcaster say good night, stealing sideways glances to see if this time others might join her heroic act, as she depicted it to herself. And thus, all her days, including all the long days of her widowhood, the days of loneliness, and afterwards in the company of hired caretakers, Mrs Yankinton would hold strictly to her noble custom, as long as her health permitted her to present herself properly in this way and her legs would carry her body which at the first became heavy, and then became smaller and smaller. But the greatest anathema to her, in any period of her life, were acts which she viewed as desecration of the flag and the singing of the anthem, and she encountered such acts over and over, for she was on the watch for them.

On that particular morning, she had to bring a certain amount of dedication to bear in this matter. In that period, our school frequently held ceremonies which were intended to create a break from the pupils' daily routine, to the point where they themselves became a certain kind of routine, and they became indistinguishable from days without ceremonies. Ceremonies on the eleventh of Adar were accompanied by praising self-sacrifice for the motherland and honouring heroes; birthdays of Herzl and Bialik, which took place first on the day itself and then later were separated so that one would not dim the glory of the other; the holiday of spring and days of independence and liberation; all these and many more were celebrated at my school, in the large courtyard, opening with a speech by the principal, and after that—always in the same order—songs and declamations. The whole time we stood in straight

lines in the open air of the large schoolyard, rain or
shine, and longed for the end of the speeches. A few parents would join us to lend festivity or importance to
those events. These were parents with a well-developed
pedagogical sense, which apparently did not include my
parents, since they never appeared at one of those ceremonies. Unlike Karni's parents, or to be precise, her
mother, Mrs Yankinton, who never missed a ceremony
or memorial day in all the years her daughter was in
school, despite the fact that there were an inordinate
number of ceremonies. And on the morning in question, Mrs Yankinton's sharp eye discerned that the boys'
classes from the adjacent school on Ahad Ha'am street,
also known as 'the boys' school', who regularly joined
our ceremonies since, as a few of our parents said, it was
a 'failing school and someone needs to give it a hand,'
did not demonstrate proper behaviour throughout the
ceremony, and especially during the singing of the
anthem. The boys moved in place, shifted their weight
from side to side, slapped each other furtively on the
back of the neck and then tried to identify the slappers,
who hurried to hide behind stronger boys' backs. Then
Mrs Yankinton's eye caught a particularly pale and bony
boy who looked more repulsive and agile than the rest,
and during the singing of the anthem his heart did not
soar but, rather, he continued to utter grunting noises
from his hiding place in order to play a prank on his
friends. Mrs Yankinton waited with a pounding heart,
lest she find herself unable to punish the youth before
the last note of the anthem died away, for running

around the schoolyard in everyone's sight, to the sounds of the anthem, was also impossible. And then, in those mere sixty seconds between the final disappearance of the last note and the principal's cry: Attention! Straight lines! At ease! Mrs Yankinton appeared, in full view of the rows of pupils, and despite the fact that she was never an expert runner, her body carried her forward cautiously but still urgently, straight ahead. And thus she managed, some thirty seconds before the end of the principal's commands, to plant a slap on the cheek of the startled renegade. After the slap, still emotional, she wiped the sweat from her brow with a large man's handkerchief, and advanced with slightly shaky steps—the effort, immeasurable both physically and psychologically, had been, in the end, too much for her—towards the small group of parents, all parents of pupils in our school and not one of them a parent of a child in the Ahad Ha'am School for Boys, who were waiting to cheer for her. Words of praise and encouragement greeted her: Good job, Esterika! Hope he'll learn his lesson! He should have gotten more! For she was one of them.

The next day I was sitting again in Karni's room. Her mother offered us, as she offered all guests, a slice of cake, a glass of sweet tea encased in a silver-plated metal sleeve for easier holding, and yet, since the metal sleeve was excellent at conducting heat, it made it impossible to hold the glass, unless the guest was trained in withstanding suffering or ready to wait until the tea had lost its warmth, and a plate of orange slices, raisins and pieces of dates spread out like a large flower on the

side. When Karni left the room to go to the bathroom
or to open the door for Zariz, the dog who scratched up
the entrance, Mrs Yankinton hurried to ask my advice:
What did I think of the new fabric she had bought in
the market? Should she make it into a skirt? A piece of
the fabric was brought as a sample. And how can I persuade Karni to wear the red dress with white polka dots
that she received from America? She begged me to use
my influence on her. I promised to try. Some years later,
Mr Yankinton invited me to a cafe in Jerusalem, where
I lived at that time, and next to a tall, black kerosene
heater that whispered quietly in a monotone (it was winter) and under pictures of artists who were once patrons
of the cafe and left their pictures to indicate either
thanks or lack of funds, among them Yosl Bergner and
Yossi Shtern, he asked me to influence Karni so that she
would not wait forever, as he said, to give birth to one
or two babies. —They have been married for five years,
he said, I am very worried. I promised to do my best to
persuade her. These were false promises. How little can
we change our friends' lives, and how little we know.
Mrs and Mr Yankinton knew only their love for their
daughter, and therefore forgot everything else. And I,
who loved her in a different way, because it was impossible to achieve a parent's way of loving, did not forget
my defects and my inability to change anything, and the
innocence I surely had then did not have the power to
cover up these flaws.

But this time Karni went down to the street because
Zariz delayed in returning from his walk, and I told

Mrs Yankinton that after my grandmother died, my mother's family almost quarrelled among themselves. I remembered with pain the argument I had recently witnessed, for it only augmented my sorrow, the sorrow which death itself brings to almost all human beings, along with its eternal incomprehensibility. Mrs Yankinton pricked up her ears: What did you say? There were arguments? What did they argue about, she wanted to know, about the flat? —No, I think they fought about Grandma's pictures and about the coffee serving set. —Pictures or drawings? Mrs Yankinton wanted to know. —Photographs, I said, and Mrs Yankinton decided to focus on the coffee service. The set included brown coffee cups, low and so thin as to be transparent, accompanied by matching cake plates which my grandmother would place, together with the cups, on the large table covered with a piece of glass and over that a yellow tablecloth, before our weekly family visits on late Shabbat mornings. An old Frigidaire electric refrigerator standing in the kitchen, whose existence in my grandmother's house was a marvel to me, as well as a source of pride which continued to buoy me in the following days, held a pitcher of coffee—placed there the day before in order not to violate the commandments of the Shabbat—which had been absorbing the chill of the electric refrigerator and which contained precise proportions of bitter coffee and sweetness, and most importantly cold which pleased us on summer days. But the cups pleased us no less than the beverage. In shades of brown, sky blue, orange, yellow and gold, a Chinese man and woman appeared—drawn with a fine brush—in traditional garb, bearing on their heads a kind of round hat which reminded me of the Christian halos I had seen in a picture book which had trailed me through my childhood. From the lowest brown band on the bottom, the colours on the cup melded into a layer of sky blue and from there to white, to yellow and to gold, and ended at the rim of the cup with a second brown band. The bands were not precise. One band seeped into the next, fell and rose again from the rim, thus conveying a certain meandering and uncertainty. And indeed, the couple, the man and the woman, appeared to sit on the edge of one band, so that only the upper part of their body was revealed to the searching eye, beyond the sky-blue stripe. They were relaxed, perhaps still loved each other after many years of marriage, despite the fact that they were no longer young. One could not be sure of that. In fact, the cups carried within them the most crucial questions: Do the man and woman love each other? What is beyond the upper brown band which has closed them in so suddenly? The cup was translucent. The more I drained my cup of coffee, the more the translucent part of the cup appeared. I moved towards the window so that the cup's transparency would be illuminated by the bright daylight and thus enter me with each swallow of coffee. In the end, only the grounds were left, a bit cloudy, like the cup's questions which no human being would ever solve. But if the two people depicted on the cup were mere householders, not lovers—then it would be better for me to die than to live . . . —And everyone wanted the coffee set for themselves? Mrs Yankinton asked, and revelled in the Poles' small-mindedness.

But in the evening the Russians came. They would come on Fridays, for then the house was wide open, as they say, for the house was always open to visitors. Years of life in the underground, outside the pleasant realm of general consensus, had taught the guests to walk the city streets with expressions of listening and worry, while looking down at the paving stones, as though they were particularly interesting, and moving along the inner part of the pavement, the one closest to fences and walls, but thus they looked like the Kirov ballet dancers who were so admired in their childhood in Russia, but whom they also left behind, for ideology was always more important than art, and one was forced to choose between them. Although even after making the correct choice, every limb of their body turned in its core to match the limbs of the dancer from Kirov, even if each part of the dancer's body was enrobed in its own unique garment; the midriff—in an Aztec-style skirt, the bust and upper arms—in a wide, woolly scarf, the head—in a tight-fitting hat like those of farmers celebrating the harvest, and the legs—in striped hose. All these garments, though they appeared so disparate one from another, nevertheless perfectly matched the body's minute movements which brought the dancer's head closer and closer to the floor and distanced it from flight. But even so, the flight did not disappear. It remained hidden and trapped in the garments, curling around each part of the body and making its movements, especially at the start of the dance, into a series of fumbling and crumpling movements. Even so, they maintained the strict regime in which the dancer, like a drawn bow, is obligated to the most precise and thought-out movements, so that when the time comes, when the bow opens and stretches, he can fly with it like an arrow that remains alone. Although the Kirov Russian dancers did not fly, they shook their arms and hands and tossed their legs to the sides and waved their fingers, meanwhile stretching their back again, the gaze straight ahead, but the garments were not discarded and the farmer's hat remained as tightly on the head as it was before, perhaps to hint that the quality of freedom is also finite, and what a small space it is which obliges us to return in the end to the normal state of modesty and restraint.

The Yankinton family's guests understood this quality of restraint but also the feeling of release and wildness which carried them like an arrow, all the way from Tzarist Russia to Mr Yankinton's study, which was turned into a guest room when needed, since the house had no living room, and it had windows, wooden closets painted black which held books, in glass-sealed showcases—Jabotinsky's entire *oeuvre* in an elegant blue binding, on whose spine, on a background of royal red, the name of the book and its author were engraved in gold: *Ze'ev Jabotinsky—Complete Writings*. Next to the books stood, on reels of tape enclosed in thin cardboard boxes, all the leader's recorded speeches. Mr Yankinton was the first to bring a real tape recorder to Israel, and he even made it available to his daughter and her friends so they could entertain themselves by listening to their voices for the first time artificially, as they sounded from outside. But, in fact, the real reason for the purchase of this expensive, clumsy Philips instrument was Jabotinsky himself, the leader and guide whose words somehow passed into eternity, or at least technological eternity, via the Philips instrument. The bookcase also held all Sholem Aleichem's writings, who, so they say, was among the leader's admirers, as well as a not-insignificant number of notebooks and writing pads. Chairs were placed beyond the bookcase and the door leading into the room, and in the centre—a Persian rug, and beyond it, Mr Yankinton's desk, also black, and massive. On the interior side of the desk, next to the windows which were open summer and winter, he sat and wrote in his journal, in which he documented all development and progress in his daughter's life. When she was an infant, he wrote every day and reported events such as flipping from her back to her stomach and onto her back again, the appearance of each tooth, then each group of teeth. After that his journal included the little one's sayings, such as: Abba, good morning! And next to it a description of the wave of the little hand. The journal was precise but not very interesting to other readers, and Mr Yankinton attached photographs which accompanied and illustrated the progress and changes which took place in a young person over time. The desk itself was also covered with photographs spread all over its broad surface, a writing surface which, as in all other homes, was under a heavy plate of glass. And Mr Yankinton would look at these photographs longingly, since they included pictures of family members who had stayed in Russia, a picture of his first child who had died of pneumonia at age 30 days, and endless photographs of his only daughter from her early birthdays, which were already in the past and seemed to him more beautiful than the days he was living through now, not least because he knew that they would never return. On the left side, on the room's southern wall, stood a wide, comfortable couch, and next to it a large radio receiver, which they would have to tap every time it fell silent to get it working again. Despite the fact that shops already sold radios with a sensitive needle which stood vertically and moved across a rectangular dial between stations until it stopped at the desired station, a radio like the one in my parents' home, Mr Yankinton clung to his old radio which was shaped like a tall chimney, with a rounded dial, the needle passing along the circumference of the circle slowly like the hands of an old pocket watch, and he did not want to hear of the possibility of exchanging it or buying a new-generation radio. Guests at the Yankinton home therefore sat on the few chairs and the wide sofa, so that the pictures of Jabotinsky hung on the walls opposite them and the black statue which showed only the leader's head and chest, placed on a black stand, were the first things their eyes fell on when their gaze settled comfortably in the space of the room after walking hunched over through the streets.

Two of the guests brought mandolins with them, another brought a balalaika. Those were the instruments preferred by their visitors: mandolins and balalaikas, and not accordions. Not even a small, elegant accordion meant for women, which was fashionable in those days and had infiltrated Tel Aviv's society salons, that is, the social meetings which took place at the homes of merchants and clerks in the city. But the soul of the guests in the Yankinton home was repelled by any form of accordion, despite the fact that it was originally the instrument which accompanied the fighters in the Russian Revolution in their hours of leisure and friendship. In the eyes of the guests on Yavneh Street, the accordion stood first of all for the hated kibbutz movement, and after that the military force which competed with Etzel—men of the Palmach in all its permutations—and finally, because of the feminine accordion, reactionism, people from Poland and the East European diaspora who immigrated to Israel in search of the good life and ignored the good of the people and the Zionist project. But when it came to singing, all these distinctions were forgotten. Most of the songs were unfamiliar to those who did not belong to the small cult. But the songs, like all the elderly fighters on their holidays, ignored this and looked back longingly on the heroism and on the war which had made a warm home for it, and sang about 'rifle will salute rifle, bullet will fire on bullet' and about expanding the borders of the homeland and about prisons where the fighters had been imprisoned in Israel and on the African continent, and this was their hour of flight when the bow was drawn back again, and again

they were unknown soldiers, ready to die and waiting
for the command. Here the rules of the general consensus were in force. No one was an outcast, no one was
held at a distance or condemned. There was no mocking
or loathing, and there was no hatred. Although they did
hate, they only hated the others, and the hatred only
accompanied them and did not permeate them, and
thus its incursion brought them closer to each other and
was justified in their eyes. But when they headed home,
an hour after midnight, they hunched over once more
and kept close to walls and fences in the deserted streets.
Sometimes the group was joined by Yakov, a theatre
actor who excelled at playing women's roles in old
farces. One of his songs was played frequently then on
the radio—against all odds, as his friends said—and was
everyone's favourite. At the meetings on Yavneh Street,
they would beg him to play the well-loved song and
would shout at him, 'Letter from Mama'!, but Yakov
would pretend not to hear. Thus, at each meeting the
pleading would last longer and Yakov would refuse
more strenuously, without even offering an explanation.
The member who brought a balalaika with him told his
friends that Yakov's personality was becoming increas-
ingly arrogant and that he was becoming more and more
like those Bolshevik pigs who stole food from the people. But the truth was that Yakov was sick of this song,
and also of his life in the theatre and his life in Israel in
general, and when he finally started singing because he
could not refuse any more, he began in a quavery voice:

Hello my child, hello from Mother
I received your letter, my good son,
And if you had known how much Mother rejoiced in it
You would have written a little more.
You wrote me that you received a ribbon
And that you are ready for the rank of corporal.
I do not understand what that means,
But if it is good, I will send you ribbons.

At these moments some of the guests teared up, and others groped with their free hands in the air towards their neighbours like a blind person seeking help from a random passer-by.

Carmi and Lani's flat in Tel Aviv was poorer than their flat in the Rechavia neighbourhood of Jerusalem, just as my parents' flat in the building with the round balconies on George Eliot Street was poorer than their first flat in Tel Aviv on Mazeh Street. I remember the flat on Mazeh Street first because of its white floor, which, unlike the floors in my friends' homes, was not decorated with geometric designs nor scattered with dark grey or black spots, so as to appear more 'interesting'. It was spread out before everyone, pure white, and it made me proud of my good luck or my parents' wise choice. I sat with my sister on the wide windowsill, the only one like it in the flat, and first we placed between us a shoebox which had been converted into a home for silkworms. Holes had been punched in the top such that air could get in but the worms could not get out, and the slender, white silkworms swelled up from all the mulberry leaves we supplied them, and became fat worms who lost their white colour and began to look slightly soiled, until they turned entirely grey, laid small eggs and turned into ugly moths. In those days, all my friends were raising silkworms, and I never went alone to the mulberry tree on Joseph HaNasi Street to collect leaves in its shade. There was always a friend ready to accompany me because her silkworms were terribly hungry. Growing silkworms was an activity which met with approval from all our parents and teachers, since it brought us closer to understanding natural processes and life cycles in general, and what was more, so they assumed, in an easy and pleasant manner. But in fact we were disgusted by the processes which revealed themselves to us, as life gave way to death so easily, and the caterpillar's cocoon stage, when it is called a pupa, did not end with hope for a more beautiful world but, rather, with the appearance of a monster-moth in the image of the Angel of Death, as he was portrayed in our childhood picture books, who would stumble about the shoebox like a lost mouse.

Over time, on the wide windowsill of plain marble, two fat silkworms crawled out of the box when I did not close the cover carefully and somehow managed to disappear entirely after jumping onto the marble—not a logical feat, to disappear on a white marble surface. But in those days people did not tend to believe in mystical phenomena as they do in our days, so those around us did not seem fazed by the disappearance of the two worms—but within a short time, the rest of the worms disappeared after them. Then the worms' place on the windowsill was occupied by a round aquarium of thick glass, containing an artificial farmhouse, coloured white and red, a sort of temple for fish lovers, with a fat gold-fish meandering about it. It was a gift I received from Mr Yankinton on my eighth birthday—one of the few birthdays which my parents marked at home, perhaps because I had just recently recovered from scarlet fever, and Mr Yankinton himself, in a short jacket and Russian gabardine trousers, carried the aquarium from his house with cautious steps, and placed it carefully on the marble windowsill to cries of wonder.

My father had been practicing for days from an old manual entitled *Exercises and Tricks for the Novice Magician*, sneaking in his hours of practice at times when we were out of the house. He then performed a surprising magic show which rested on two tricks: the spinning knife trick, in which a lump of dough which was stuck to one side, in full view of all, appeared to be on both sides or did not appear at all; and the disappearing card trick, for which, in order to execute it properly, he donned a shirt with long sleeves and made sure to leave one sleeve partially unbuttoned, since he had not yet entirely mastered this illusion.

In the flat on Mazeh Street, I once tore a piece of white paper from my drawing pad and rolled it tightly in order to shove it into one of the openings of the electric socket on the wall next to my bed. I knew that a hump-backed witch, wrapped in snail slime, would immediately come out of it to reprimand me, but I was not entirely sure and wanted to check. But no witch appeared. Instead, my body shook and a white being came and enfolded me. I crawled away and was saved, however, and never said anything about it to my parents. And outside the western window, where the building's outer wall made a corner with the neighbours' flat, two of Mrs Koris' nephews then came out on the balcony. These two had been hired at that time as actors in the Municipal Theatre after surviving the hardships of the war, for although the entire Koris family had come here long before and become wealthy in the lumber business, the two nephews had remained in Romania and endured more difficult times than other Romanians, since they were Jewish, and at the end of the war they had arrived here, to live initially with their aunt, but they did not join the family lumber business since they were drawn to the arts, and in that field, like all the Koris family, they achieved success and fame, and when they were hired by the theatre, one of them played famous lovers like Romeo, since he was considered a handsome man with his black hair pulled back, like a Spaniard, and the second played what were called character roles and appeared in A View from the Bridge and Death of a Salesman in the role of the father and also in A Man for All Seasons. But when they were still young, when publicity and fame, or lack of them, did not sully their mood, they would come out to the small balcony—where their aunt, Mrs Koris, hung the family's laundry summer and winter, hung it or took it down, and thus spent many hours every day on that small balcony which bordered our flat and created a right angle with the western window of our bedroom, and though the balcony had a roof, the laundry was not under its shelter but, rather, hung in the open air under the heavens, and therefore more than once she would have to scramble to remove it from the clothesline before the rain fell harder, as big, fat drops were already beginning to wet it, or to bring it inside the house before it became entirely dried out in the hot desert wind and then 'all of you would feel its pricking on your body'. And Mrs Koris would hurriedly stuff the still partially wet laundry into a large basin so it could dry comfortably there—in order to polish all the pairs of shoes which they had bought thinking to please the girls, and every time they went out they would wear a different pair which sometimes had two colours, like black and white, which made them harder to clean, and they would brush with broad movements of the elbows and arms, all the while singing in Romanian.

Years later, my sister happened to be invited to that small flat on Mazeh Street when she accompanied her lawyer husband to obtain the signature of the son of a long-time client, who was at that time in France, on some warranty document. And thus, after many years, completely by chance, my sister saw our childhood home again, in which nothing had remained as it once was, and the white floor had been replaced by fashionable parquet, and the son of the long-time client, a wealthy urban-dweller by nature, nevertheless knew to value the flat's hidden beauty, since he himself had bought it from people who were completely unknown to us. And suddenly, through the western window which faced the wall of the neighbours' flat and their small balcony, my sister saw Mrs Koris, in the same pose of caution and worry which had always marked her when she hung up or took down wet clothes from the line, hanging the family's laundry which, however, had shrunk considerably from the time when her nephews polished their shoes on that balcony, since the family's only son had left, the nephews had become famous actors who had received good reviews and had grown old in the theatre until they died, and Mrs Koris herself had been a widow for several decades. The quantity of laundry had therefore lessened, but it was still laundry, and one needed to supervise it lest it get rained on. And Mrs Koris, with the same white hair as in my childhood and the same small, worried hands, hung up one more load of laundry.

Compared to the flat on Mazeh Street, our new home on George Eliot Street seemed like poor living quarters. Aside from the name of the street, which testified to a certain greatness because of its foreign ring, and because the determined spirit of a female genius was always present there, and the name was mentioned by my mother, when asked for her address, with a certain contempt directed at the interlocutor, since she expected his response: Wha-a-a-t? Georgio Roth? which showed that he had never even heard of the celebrated author, had never read a book by her, and did not know that, even back in the nineteenth century, she had taken a man's name as a form of protest. Indeed, most of those who asked my mother's address did not know who George Eliot was and who wrote *Weaver of Raveloe*, for most public servants, such as clerks in the health clinic or in various departments of the National Insurance Institute, did not find time to read books because of the difficulties life placed before them, and they were the ones assigned to fill out forms and ask questions, but mainly, my mother was already older, almost elderly, in those days when she began chafing against the world, in her days of discreet widowhood, and she grew older with each passing day and week, while those who asked questions and filled out forms, the clerks behind the counters of public-hospital clinics and local bank branches, were young people of working age between twenty and forty, and names of people from the previous century, or the century before that, no matter how famous they were in their time, did not stir them at all. But except for George Eliot, the flat to which we moved had nothing to recommend it. The house on Mazeh Street spoke of lost splendour to anyone who spent time there, visited briefly, or even glanced at it in passing. The pool of pure water in the entrance garden, which had been home to—and had been built specially for—two goldfish who could dive under the clear water and come to the surface whenever someone passed by the pool, was now without water or fish, a dry pool, though still a pool and not a solid expanse of asphalt; the radiators which ceased to work after the war; the low steps,

rounded at the edges, in the spacious entrance lobby and
between each floor, all of these caused the pleasant, care-
free days to linger in the interior of the building and its
nine flats, just as the poverty and echoes of distress settled in the building on George Eliot Street in every one
of its ten flats, divided into two entryways, Entryway
A—the front one and therefore slightly more prestigious—and Entryway B, deeper in the courtyard, which
became a hideout for street cats, for there they received
their only meal of the day from a good-hearted woman.
The kitchens on George Eliot Street shared a common
balcony with the neighbours on the same floor, and my
parents, who felt the need to preserve a modicum of pri-
vacy, set up a dividing wall with the aid of several empty
kerosene cans, a bucket and two brooms. It was not the
materials, however, but the mere fact of setting up a bar-
ricade which hurt the neighbours' pride and became an
ongoing source of insult, since they took it as a sign of
arrogance and alienation. In that same kitchen, cabinets
hung on rickety hinges, their original green colour covered with an indistinct patina of passing time, and like
the cabinets, their contents all testified to previous lives,
when that same kitchen had offered itself simultaneously to three families who shared the rooms of the flat,
and the desolation of the bath and toilet testified to the
members of those same three families who shared the
line to the toilet, the shower and the kitchen, and all of
them promised me that from now on they would be my
close companions, and only the obscure sound of the
boats, the sound of a siren which began and ended as if

it had no beginning and no end, and which I heard only in the George Eliot flat which looked out towards the far-off sea, from a height at which every picture becomes possible, including a picture of a steamship with three black smokestacks, never reached me again in any other flat, even though I searched for it in the many other flats I lived in in my life and was comforted by its existence as a sound which lodged itself inside of me because it left the world behind.

Carmi and Lani, my maternal uncle and aunt, also left their spacious flat in the Rehavia neighbourhood of Jerusalem, which, adjoining the courtyard, was surrounded by trees and green shrubs flowering outside its windows, and moved to a sorrow-steeped flat in Tel Aviv on Nachmani Street next to Petah Tikva Way. Though trouble had dogged my uncle's life in Jerusalem as well, since his wife relentlessly battered him with condemnations and accusations, and her style became more barbed and ironic as time passed, with the experience and skill acquired in all her years of marriage, until my Uncle Carmi grew weary of his life and went to consult with the Rebbe of Gur, whom he served and admired, who lived at that time in Jerusalem. No pious Jew, and certainly not a rabbi, can recommend divorce, and therefore the Rebbe of Gur listened quietly to my Uncle Carmi's words, and after a few moments of thought, suddenly announced in a clear voice: You have no wife! Shortly after these events, my uncle fell ill with a strange malady, from which he ultimately died, and thus the rabbi's mysterious words came true, words which many interpreted as prophecy. But perhaps they were not prophecy, and they meant something else.

We used to come to Carmi and Lani's flat during the long days of the festival weeks. The narrow hallway where my aunt received us with joyful cries led to the living room which was the room intended for show, and on an old Persian carpet stood a heavy table, six chairs and a tablecloth covered with tassels which served as a sort of decoration. My aunt called, still in her joyful voice, Carmi! Carmi! Come out! Come to your guests! Aunt Lani walked us into the living room and called again: Carmi! Carmi! Come here! From afar could be heard the sound of a radio being turned on and off, and still we sat as guests whom no one comes to greet, though not in the host's bad graces, but finding themselves embarrassed because they are causing embarrassment. I thought to myself that my aunt does not usually have such a joyful voice. I remembered the many fights with her husband which I had unwillingly witnessed and the trip to Jerusalem with my other aunt, Gina, my father's sister. Five years had passed since then. Then I was a plump, rosy-cheeked girl under my black hair, and now I was a slim girl, tall for my age, and my face—it was as though something had been taken from it. What was it? What was I searching for even then, which was found in every passer-by who welcomedd me with a few moments' kindness, offering a few predictable questions and some casual chat before going on his way. Already then my soul was desolate, and later I found this kindness, though not fully, between the pages of books sold on the second floor of a shop, all of them by English and American publishers, in glossy wrappers; song books, picture albums and literary quarterlies bound in evergreen. Browsing was permitted. But the kindness did not transfer itself to me, it merely lingered next to me in a language unaccustomed but open to discovery, it forbade me to spread its secret which I could not know anyway, and to publicize our hasty meetings. I bought a few literary pamphlets and hid them in the house, wrapped in plain brown paper. This did not bring redemption, but it was sort of pronouncing a verdict, as is done at every border crossing (my sister who rapidly uncovered my secret said: What are you thinking, going around with your nose in the air, so special ever since you bought those pamphlets?). A few leaps by goats who came from the distant green forest, the evergreen forest, beyond the boulders, and only a few of them survived. I took a seat on a heavily upholstered chair in the home of my ultra-orthodox uncle and aunt. The sounds of an argument between the brother and sister could be heard from behind the closed door. The sister, in the faint voice of a young virgin: Don't you dare turn that on! It is *muktze*! The brother: It is not! Stupid! It is the middle of a festival week! Again a radio could be heard, secular songs by listener request were heard and then abruptly shut off. The last song played for no more than ten seconds. I identified it as a nostalgic song in which a young man calls his lover to leave everything and follow him. I tried to lose myself in the song, for the words and melody pleased me, but the sister would not permit this. She showed great firmness. The walls of the living room displayed photographs of great rabbis from different periods, and among them the Rebbe of Gur stood out, dressed in a festive silk capote, white with stripes, and crowned with a large fur hat. It was not right to listen to secular songs by listener request in such a house, not even on the intermediate days of the festival. But my cousin, Carmi's oldest son, was addicted to the radio and did not like studying. Behind the closed doors of the children's and parents' rooms, neglect reigned. My Aunt Lani had just enough strength to clean and straighten up the living room, perhaps guests might come. And we can manage with the dirt, and when Papa will earn enough, like other fathers earn, we will hire a cleaning lady to come twice a week, not once every two weeks like we do now. In the meantime, three years had passed since the family moved from the Rechavia neighbourhood of Jerusalem to Tel Aviv, and matters had not improved. My aunt straightened the edges of the tablecloth slightly and placed the tassels diagonally as a decoration. She could not bear the sounds of arguing and the radio being switched off and on in the closed room. Every evening they speak peacefully to each other, she explained, they are planning what to do tomorrow, Carmi! she continued in the same tone but a higher voice, in fact extremely high, Why aren't you coming? You have guests, I told you!! Aunt Lani went into the kitchen to put on the kettle and the door of the side room opened. Carmi appeared there, dressed in an unkempt robe with his hair uncombed, his face puffy. He was already weary of not earning enough, not earning like everyone else. Many creditors had already visited him in his shop next to the Romano Building. In the evenings, he would appear at our house for frantic consultations and my father would bring him into the third room and give him advice, all for nought. —Close the shop, people don't buy from wholesalers nowadays. Anyone who wants to make money has to go into retail (Carmi's and my mother's parents had owned a retail shop in the Polish village). Do you think it's easier to manage a factory? My father also wanted to complain, but Carmi came to our house evening after evening and continued to hole up in the third room with my father until all my father's lines of defence were breached. In the end, he signed a promissory note, something that caused my mother many a sleepless night, and almost caused us to find ourselves out on the street, turning our flat back over to the landlord in exchange for a sum no greater than a day labourer's annual salary. After he signed the promissory note for my uncle (my father kept a signed copy for himself in the silver-plated cigarette case that was put out for guests, placing it on the other side of the screened barrier which divided the case in two), my father's tranquillity was also shattered and his gaze deepened. My uncle's illness—though it was of a different sort, all diseases share common origins—struck him too, though in its own way, since like the rest of its kin, it always preferred to settle deep inside the homes of the poor.

My Uncle Carmi fell ill in the winter of that year. But while we were still visiting his home, he would appear at the entrance to the couple's bedroom, looking tattered, his face unkempt as if he came from a fight and not from sleep—it was not his life which was abandoning him but that he was abandoning his life rapidly, for he had come to understand that he would never again be desired by those who surrounded him all the time, whom he had not the strength to leave, for they were to him his life, for whom, in order to delight them, with bare hands—for he did not take the time to find a pair of suitable gloves—he would create large snowballs to throw at them, he was in such a hurry to make them happy. Children! he called, it snowed again in Jerusalem! Being theatrical and loving the homeland, he indicated to his children the source of the snow with the word 'Jerusalem', though in truth he viewed the source of the snow as something divine in the fullest sense of the word, for God, as he believed according to what was written in the Bible, holds the key to the treasure houses of ice and snow and sometimes opens them. How joyful it was then with his children, whose hair was fair like Gentile children's hair, and he too, such a bearded Gentile with a yarmulke, happy and well-liked by men and women, but now no more. He comforted himself that all this would change in the next world.

A return to the past, which one sometimes finds in films that offer various means to go back in time, mostly via trails of murky magic leading to some past period which has frozen momentarily to take us in again, like the figures of the actors, entirely naturally, exactly as we were then, or similarly, apocalyptic visions directing us towards the future, towards the time which is after time and after the destruction of the earth, the human beings on it, and all its civilizations—in the end, both these movements lead us precisely to ourselves just as we are now at this fleeting moment, just as the immutability of the Olympic gods and their adventurous victories led the ancient Greeks to themselves and not to the gods, to their own fleeting moment, out of which they drew their aspiration for that which they would never possess.

Gods, like the past, will ultimately leave us alone, frustrated with our longings, because of too much loneliness, because of the deep-seated recognition that we are incapable of getting anywhere, because of the anger and the pity and the reconciliation, and alongside them the knowledge that these too will soon pass away and, like a blind moth in flight, we will not see the vision towards which we are hurling ourselves with all our might and too fast for ourselves, but not fast at all in human terms, and certainly not in divine terms, to see beauty whose like has never been seen, and therefore it has never been, with empty eyes over enormous vistas such as those between the door and this window, the one which is always closed, and I step forward to open it.

The noise of a crowd always filled the Yankinton family's living room when evening fell, at the end of a long Friday. But even before it arrived, when weariness had not yet overtaken us, and Sofa Knizhnikov came to school at the final bell to meet Karni, her friend who was two years her junior, I joined them with the dubious feeling common to all those who are extraneous. Karni would occasionally drag me as escort on visits to Sofa's house, and I would hear, while still at the flat entrance, the slam of the thin door to the inner room where Mrs Knizhnikov barricaded herself against us. And just as the sound of the classroom bell—which, like children in educational institutions throughout the world, we called 'the saving bell'—proclaimed the passage from boredom to alertness and a certain anticipation of a prolonged school break which would not finish, as it usually did, at the end of the day, since it was the eve of a holy day, nor at the end of a tedious holy day which would leave us when three stars winked in the sky. Rather, the school break would stretch out over what would come after the Shabbat, and after all the divisions into Sabbaths and secular days which would come from now on, for in the loved and desired world there would no longer be such Sabbaths that make us long for their ends—thus proclaimed the quiet click of Mrs Knizhnikov's door, though with the opposite intention, heralding a new understanding that our freedom would never be limitless, there would always be some door closing before us and some ear for which the lively, charming chatter of three cute girls, as we saw ourselves—grating voices of vulgarity and stupidity. I respected Sonia Knizhnikov's closed door, but I did not want to open it and take my place with her in the regions of loneliness and suffering, whose existence, though not their power, I could only suppose.

Sofa spoke of buying shoes. Being two years older than us, she visited shops freely and always earned the salesladies' trust—Sofa knew how to greet people pleasantly whose names she did not know—but she had no money. —I tried on about ten pairs of shoes, she said, and I found fault with each shoe, and the dumb saleswoman would go and bring me another pair. Just at that moment Sofa's mother opened her door and requested: Girls, don't laugh so loudly. After that she came out anyway to fix us cookies on a large plate and orange juice in glasses, and Karni recounted how Sofa's mother had already tried twice to kill herself in the bathroom. She slit her wrists and the water was full of blood, and she was naked. Sonia Knizhnikov served us a large plate where she had placed a tower of chocolate-filled cookies in the centre and surrounded it with blood-red Aviva candies. The red-candy coating, hard as an eggshell, melted in your mouth, and contained a potent paste of milk chocolate, like Mrs Knizhnikov's face and her hair tightly framing it, dark hair pulled back off her forehead and from the right side, beyond the part, with a girl's barrette. On that Friday which was leaving the world, I could not see Mrs Knizhnikov's face without seeing her lying naked in the bathtub in bloody water. —Offer your friends juice, Sofa's mother said to her daughter, for she wanted to save herself the effort. Now everything was difficult for her. For two weeks already she had not done laundry or cleaned the rooms. Sofa only told us that later, after the fact, when she was already an adult. And Sonia Knizhnikov, who did not try again to commit suicide, moved herself through the days and sometimes went to movies with her friend, Mrs Yankinton, for Mr Yankinton detested the invention of the cinema and clung to his simple stills camera, until she was trapped by her illness, and from then on she scarcely left her flat and just sat by the window, quietly watching the passers-by and the funerals which would rush past down the street to Hadassah Hospital, with the mourners yelling and the women keening loudly, and after that everything disappeared except for the silence, which became heavier.

Sonia Knizhnikov watched all these and her gaze became distant. First she grew fat, and then very thin. She refused treatment—even though in those days, like nowadays, there was really no effective treatment for that illness—and just continued to shrink until she became tiny. And people recognized her only by her place at the window but did not want to look in her direction again.

I could not know all these things when the candy's red eggshell dissolved in one's mouth before the chocolate ball even appeared, when the inside of one's mouth was already stained red, and even the outside of one's mouth bore signs of a pleasure that had passed, and my friend Karni said to me, Oy, we are late for Heitzen! Thus we ran downstairs and crossed the empty street to arrive again at the house on Yavneh Street, where we were supposed to meet the piano teacher at 3 in the afternoon. My friend Karni named the teacher Heitzen upon scrambling and reforming the letters of the teacher's original name, Nitza. But to me, Heitzen really was the Queen of the Wilderness, a character from the book *Letters Talk*, which I read during my illness. Her skeletal thinness, her dry skin, made her similar to the queen who represented the Hebrew letter *tzaddi*, and she was in fact the spokeswoman for the Queen of the Wilderness in the real world, for this queen, like Heitzen, came from the desolate desert populated not by human beings but by letters, and these letters do not join up to form pleasant words or stories but, rather, live separately one from the other in order to devote themselves to the research which occupies most of their time, for they thirst to explore their origins and their various roles in language and in grammar, and they gain thereby more pleasure than from anything else. And not a few books have been written in the wake of this research, and they fill the desert.

When we arrived at the Yankinton flat on Yavneh Street, Heitzen was already sitting on Mr Yankinton's black office couch. She glared at us because of our tardiness but she was not actually angry. Heitzen did not love her work, particularly when she had to teach two girls at the keyboard of one piano, so the abbreviated lesson, which had come about without her intervention, was

only welcome, and what is more, Mr Yankinton strove
to make her waiting time pleasant and did so, as he usually did, with self-deprecating humour which did not
cross the bounds of good taste. Thus, for example, he
apologized profusely on our accounts for the tardiness,
as though we could not help being late since otherwise,
we would have had to refuse the Queen after she invited
us to a game of cricket, and to leave the game in the middle would have insulted the Queen and the other play-
ers, isn't that so? he sought Heitzen's confirmation.
Heitzen did not smile. Being herself a queen, albeit
Queen of the Wilderness, she knew that in a miserly
desert like hers one did not squander smiles easily. But
it pleased her that Mr Yankinton tried so hard. Though
suddenly he leapt out of his seat: How can I be speaking
with Madame while I am not appropriately dressed in
her honour? And indeed it was a hot day, and, in the
small flat in Tel Aviv, the heat was an expected compan-
ion, and Mr Yankinton, in an open shirt, suddenly hurried, much more than one would expect from such a
man, for he acted out of a certain delicate criticism of
bourgeois habits, to button up his shirt precisely, the
shirt which the heat had forced him to unbutton only
an hour earlier, and then we arrived. Despite her glow-
ering face, Heitzen was in a good mood, and remained
so for the rest of that day. At an upright piano, black, not
tuned for years, on a summer's day, sat a thin, stooped
woman with unkempt hair who leaned more and more
heavily on the keyboard. We sat on either side of her,
and Heitzen played a simple piece, easily remembered,

with two hands, and then we were asked to repeat it, each one playing a different hand. I was assigned to play the left hand, but I did not fulfil my mission well. Karni was assigned to repeat the performance of the right hand and she, blessed with a better ear than mine, executed it much more successfully. Heitzen's cries rang out from time to time: Louder! Louder! Girls, watch! Do you see this note? It is the note Sol, and it should be all the way to the floor!! She struck the key forcefully again and again. —To the floor! The key was destined to get there and we were being required to help it. I looked at the yellow-brown floor, ornamented with a geometric pattern which I did not like, as though the colours were encroaching on each other with sharp feelers, and it was far from the note Sol and from all the keys. It was minding its own business. I understood that the key was not going to reach the floor, not only because it was far away, but mostly because all the keys were enclosed in the wooden envelope of the piano. I understood that Heitzen was asking us to think of the key as if it were trying to touch the floor and as if all the other keys were also trying to touch the floor. I knew it was impossible, but the keys had ferocious ambition. Heitzen played everything twice and with great courage. At the end of each lesson, to show off, she would also play us a polonaise by Chopin. How powerful were those polonaises. Only as an adult did I learn to recognize, mainly in the playing of the still-youthful Rubenstein, their beauty and bitterness. They were polonaises. How sad the history of a people, how terrible the past which is gone,

even when it is presented in its splendour. In the year
in which I studied with Karni under Heitzen, I did not
develop a love of music. My achievements remained
pathetic. I did acquire a certain skill in my left hand but
it was not enough. Karni, who developed the right hand
in her playing, later used it in playing flute, which she
learnt on her own, in the shadow of Heitzen's far-off
teaching. When we tried to play the short pieces which
we practiced ad nauseum—together, as if we ourselves
were the two hands of a single person—we were like
two geese trying, despite the heavy body, to spread their
wings and thus escape their fate, the urging of the young
gooseherd, a light bamboo staff in her hand, as she was
leading the flock to the summit of a low hill. We practiced over and over but no piece came out sounding
decent. Mr and Mrs Yankinton, who had provided the
piano where the lessons had taken place, and had also
brought Heitzen to us, perhaps out of pity, and perhaps
it was Mr Yankinton who selected her from among his
ever-widening circle of acquaintances, for that reason
itself, they allowed her to make us believe that it is possible to play with only one hand if you do not have the
money to pay for a lesson in which you will be taught
to play with two hands, a lesson dedicated just to you.
Yet, so Heizen believed, it is possible even with one hand
to awaken the musical ability which is innate in everyone, but sometimes is dormant and under-developed, as
she told us. And so they allowed her teach us to listen
only to thundering sounds, in order to awaken this dormant ability, and not to hear the whispery, dark sound

of the music, appreciate the harmonies, and disdain strident sounds or even eschew them entirely. They allowed her to let our two hands play—Karni's right and my left—each one to herself, as two separate people, as we actually were, and mostly, they allowed her to fetter our musical taste for years to come.

But Mr Yankinton strove to perfect his daughter's education in every way possible, basing it not only on Beitar values, important as they were, perhaps even infinitely important, but also on universal values accepted by the world, which included art appreciation and knowledge of European languages. Therefore Mr and Mrs Yankinton spoke Russian with their daughter, and when she got older, her mother taught her to read the Cyrillic alphabet. But it was also important to know additional languages, and Mr Yankinton, lacking faith in the effectiveness of a public-school education, as well as financial means, discerned in Ms Borochin a potentially excellent English teacher and offered her a position of one hour a week teaching two girls who also happened to be good friends. Ms Borochin was about forty at that time, as it seems to me looking back, though in my school days I saw her as an old woman whose frantic fascination with choosing the right spouse, which she shared with us, did not jive at all with her appearance. She seemed to me like a woman from one of the Chaplin movies I had seen during the holidays, since in those days older Israelis assumed that Chaplin movies were for children and therefore the cinema screened them daily for us.

With her tightly gathered hair and sharp features, Ms Borochin did not strike me as a pretty woman. She lived in the 'Pioneers' House' on King George Street opposite the first Beitar headquarters. Mr Yankinton, who told us that immediately, went on to advise us to treat Ms Borochin respectfully and prepare all the homework assignments that she would give us, and to remember that, as a new immigrant with no relatives in Israel, she was forced to live in the Pioneers' House and share her room with another woman. But we, who heard all these things and made the required promises— found it hard to keep our word. Ms Borochin first taught us about adverbs in English, a part of speech which we found difficult to understand even in Hebrew, and anyway we still had two more years before we would learn grammar rules in Hebrew, but Ms Borochin, who viewed us in a certain way as small friends, and perhaps because she lacked another outlet, also shared with us her ongoing dilemmas regarding which men were suitable for her and which would she do well to prefer. We learnt English with Ms Borochin for a year, and at the end of that year, after we had learnt, albeit at a distance, the qualities of infinite numbers of men, some bald and some bewigged, impersonating professors of osteology, a magician and performer of magic tricks named Yoki (whom, by the way, Ms Borochin herself joined several times in his shows as an assistant, and once also as a young woman whose body was sawed in two), gardeners specializing in medicinal herbs, and one hypnotist. All these, she told us, she rejected because they only took advantage of her. I did not understand what it meant that they all took advantage of her, for how was it possible to exploit a woman who did not have any property (I remembered Mr Yankinton telling us about her room in the Pioneers' House). But in the end, just before the year was out, Ms Borochin finally told us that she had met a serious man, formerly a dance teacher in his native Hungary, who had immigrated to Israel, and until he opened his own dance school, he was looking for work as a ballroom dance teacher in one of the existing schools. Thus, simply but respectfully, she described the occupation and profession of her expected groom. For several weeks we heard about the good looks and generous heart of this dance teacher, who himself became engaged during those weeks, and only at the beginning of the summer did it all suddenly end, and Ms Borochin, who by then had already asked us many times, 'How it will be to marry someone so much older than me who can no longer go up the stairs quickly?', found out that she had been deceived. This time she cried almost the whole lesson and was so weak that she did not mention the disgusting adverb even once. —The Hungarian dance teacher turned out to be a villain, she said, he did not take advantage of her the way others did but in a much more cruel way. And he deceived me, she said, for not saying everything and hiding the truth is called deceiving, girls. And he did not tell me that he has heart disease and that he has had two heart attacks, and that when he feels bad—short of breath or something—he has to put a pill under his tongue immediately. And thus

the Hungarian dance teacher became a persona non
grata, and in a way that we did not quite understand, we
were expected from now on to feel deep contempt for
this man, whom up to now we had been taught to like
and admire, only because he was found to be sick and
wretched. I could not understand Ms Borochin's great
wrath in this matter, expressed by scathing words such
as 'villain' and 'swindler', for normally she was a well-
mannered woman who was anxious to train us to be cul-
tured people who would one day come out in society.
But like Heitzen's lessons, Ms Borochin's lessons were
almost fruitless, if one judged them, looking back, as
lessons intended to improve our knowledge of English.
For in this sphere they provided no discernable achievement, and what prevented such achievement more than
anything was not Ms Borochin's stories about the men
in her life, nor her emotions which wandered among
them. The main failure was ours, and it was born in us
and returned to us, and it was what made us unable to
focus on the teacher's explanations, not just about the
adverb but also about the character and shape of all the
verbs and nouns and various parts of speech and their
rules in the English language. For not only thoughts,
associations and various feelings, the honk of car horns,
the shuffling feet and sounds of wailing from passing
funerals, distracted us from our teacher's droning voice.
There was another factor, less predictable, which
befogged our senses. Sometimes a momentary exchange
of glances was enough to light the short fuse of the
upsurge which arose in us. It started in the depths, when

it was still under our control, at least somewhat, when self-restraint became the our most valuable possession, or at least a quality to strive for, and the frequent bouts of choking which attacked us then indicated that this quality, like all the other qualities which human beings strive to achieve, was not within our reach. Then the hidden upsurge surfaced as loud laughter which swept everything away in its wake. Karni was the first one who spouted forth the laughter, and then I joined her. At these moments the door to the study would open and Mr Yankinton would turn to us severely and sadly, but we could not get hold of ourselves, however much we wanted to. For it would seem to us that the laughter was waning away and we would already assume that it was finished and done with, but we were two. As long as one is busy with his own internal housekeeping and controls his own timing, he governs himself in his own soul's domain, but we were two and the spark of laughter in us had not been entirely extinguished. All it took, therefore, was for our eyes to meet, or the teacher's careless hand movement in which, intending to reach for the lighter to light herself another cigarette, she would instead reach for the small box of pencil sharpeners which looked to her like a lighter, for the spark of mirth to once again ignite a surge of wild laughter. In this way, the lesson dwindled away, and Ms Borochin, who felt that her income was no longer guaranteed in this house, wiped the lines of grammar and reading off her face, and read a series of sentences which would serve us in due time to carry on idle polite conversation with English speakers in a more refined way, in 'natural English', as Ms Borochin was wont to say, eyeing us with a pitying gaze which said that we would never reach this high plain of 'natural English', no matter how hard we tried. But one must try anyway. Society does not forgive slackers, and of course we wanted to be accepted into S-o-c-i-e-t-y when the time came. We were silent with shame. From her bag, Ms Borochin then withdrew a page inscribed with a few sentences which she had prepared the day before. The first one read: '*I beg your pardon, what did you say?*' and she read it out loud to us a few times, until Mr Yankinton opened the door again, this time out of concern, for his cautious senses told him that the English lesson had changed direction. Like sheep we bleated after her: '*I beg your pardon, what did you say?*' and we were assigned to practice the sentence at home. But we were categorically forbidden to write this sentence. —Now only using your ears, everything aurally, said Ms Borochin.

The sentence I learnt in my English lessons with Karni stayed with me for years and never left my memory. But I did not manage to make proper use of it. From time to time I would utter it in company, to the point where I was suspected of being deaf, and someone once commented to me that I spoke too polished, artificial English and advised me to use this phrase the next time I have tea with the Queen, if I ever receive such an invitation. Moreover, my pronunciation was imprecise.

Since we had been forbidden to write the sentence, I spoke it as I had heard it, bastardized: 'pargen' instead of 'pardon'. And once more, years passed before I managed to convey the meaning of the sentence in a simple, natural expression of asking pardon in English.

When the lesson was over, Mr Yankinton opened his wrinkled black leather wallet and paid Ms Borochin her wages as he accompanied her to the door. Then he returned to us: That's not the way, he said. That's no way to treat a person, even more so a poor woman who goes from house to house in this heat for the miserable pennies she receives. You really must change. I do not know if Mr Yankinton's words caused me to change, but I was immediately grateful for them, for even if he was scolding us, he did not do so in the way that most adults scold children. His words were direct, as if he, like us, was liable to fail and scorn those weaker than us, those who had little or nothing. But more important and valuable to me, though I only recognized it looking back, was that his words filled me with a new kind of understanding; I knew that I had my father and mother, that Ricky was my sister and that Karni had her own parents and a dog. And all my other friends had parents and brothers and sisters and grandfathers and grandmothers. All this was correct and therefore justified. But I never thought that the other people, those who existed for themselves and not just for us, have their own lives in which we do not take up much space. Ms Borochin comes to teach us because of the money Mr Yankinton pays her at the end of each lesson and not because of us, and without this money she would not last, not in the Pioneers' House or anywhere else, and she would have to live in the street or in Meyer Park. I was flustered and saddened at the thought that I had, without even thinking about it, hastened the day when Ms Borochin would have to live in the city streets or sleep on a bench in Meyer Park. I planned to approach the teacher at the beginning of the next lesson and beg her pardon, and perhaps even utter the words in English, 'I beg your pargen, what did you say?' in the most polished way I could at that time, but we had no more lessons with Ms Borochin. Mr Yankinton announced to us that she had married her dentist and gone off with him for an extended honeymoon, so he said, to Cypress.

And thus arrived the late hours of a Friday afternoon. The quiet which suddenly filled the air brought with it sadness and celebration, since it was comprised of what is no longer and what has left us; noise, sounds of laughter, footsteps, telephone conversations, all these were silenced and thus missing from the space which then enwrapped us, which was part of our human existence, and all these were voices from the here and now, which populated our memory, leaving us quiet in which to think about them. But I did not want to think about them. I looked at the window of the Yankinton home, the same window where Mr Yankinton was leaning, waiting for his daughter to return from a Scouts meeting or the ice-cream shop on Allenby, and now I saw reflected in it the diminutive figure of Gaga Gorochov approaching from the end of the street, heading towards the house on Yavneh Street.

Gaga Gorochov bore one of the most famous names in the Hebrew Labour movement. Gorochov was the movement's ideologist and had written ten volumes of articles and essays. But Gaga Gorochov was very far from the Labour ideology, and the proximity of the name did not say anything about her own leanings, devoted entirely to the values of the Beitar movement and its spinoffs. Gaga admired and loved Mr Yankinton. In the absence of Jabotinsky, the unshakable leader who was no longer among the living, she felt it proper to revere his successor, as Mr Yankinton appeared to her. Jabotinsky's collected works, in gold lettering behind the glass doors of his bookcase, were enough to convince her that she was in a kind of shrine. She was fortunate to have met such an accomplished man who was passing his creative life in the shadow of the statues of the leader, who had founded the Institute and the Museum for Research on Ze'ev Jabotinsky and the Beitar movement, and now ran both institutions, and moreover he was Mr Yankinton, always ready to lend her an ear. And thus it was that every Friday, two hours before all the other friends gathered, she would come to Yavneh Street and Mr Yankinton would closet himself with her in his office. Mrs Yankinton would serve sweet tea with a slice of cake alongside it, and Mr Yankinton would reminisce about his childhood in Russia, and afterwards his days as a young man, a rebel and a Zionist

in the days of the Tzar. There were so many revolution-
aries then, he would tell her, that they could not figure
out which kind of revolutionary I was, but they jailed
me anyway, just to be on the safe side. And then he
would recount the terrible snowstorm that hit him,
when he was sure that his life had come to an end.
And thus passed hours or perhaps only minutes, the
storm was so terrible. And when it eased a bit and he
emerged from the whirlwind, he discovered that he was
standing at the entrance to his house. Then he said: I
walked many kilometres on foot, and I could barely
walk, and it took tremendous effort. And all that time I
was walking in a circle. And then Gaga told him how
much she loved Ze'ev Jabotinsky, and how much she
admired him, Mr Yankinton, for he is the only one in
this country who numbers among his own treasures all
Ze'ev's speeches in the leader's own voice. And she told
him of how, when they had just arrived in Israel, four
people were crowded into one room in the Shikun
Vatikim, her parents and the two children, she and her
brother Judah, and how Judah married young and left
them to start his own family, and all his time now is
devoted to the genre of traditional Israeli music which
he prefers over his original family, so she feels, over his
parents and sister, since he devotes almost endless time
to it, and of course focuses particularly on the songs of
underground, and up to now he has already founded five
choirs in Gush Dan and the South and he conducts
them without pay, thus passing on Beitar values to
future generations, and it is just a shame that he allots

so little time for his parents who particularly need care now. And the fact that she is always at their disposal, that is of course understood. But Judah Gorochov is something else, he has become a celebrity. And then she recounts how she was so close to Judah when they were children in Russia, and once, when they were chasing each other around the dinner table, the lamp fell on them. Perhaps the noise they made and the pounding of their feet loosened the lamp from the ceiling, and when it fell, its metal point struck the top of Gaga's skull and her parents took her to the hospital. There they shaved the area, cleaned it and stitched the wound, without anesthetic, Gaga said, because at that time they were saving those materials for the front, and ever since, no hair has grown in that place and I wear a wig. Mr Yankinton reassures her that it is not at all noticeable. At these moments he wants to go up and hug her and bring her close to his large body, but he continues to sit on the other side of the black desk and listen.

My brother Judah caused me this bald spot when he was a child, though not on purpose, and afterwards got married and left the house and researched Israeli folk songs while I continued to take care of our parents, and even today I continue to do so, and in the evening I return to my room to make myself a supper of beans and soup, and after that I wash all the clothes I wore that day, of course, first underwear and then blouse, skirt and stockings and the thin sweater, I wash everything, and every new day I wear completely clean clothes and I hang up the wet ones in the courtyard, for I live on the ground floor, and the intimate garments—Gaga meant the belt she wore during menstruation—I hang under the skirt so that passers-by will not notice it. Gaga opened her heart to Mr Yankinton, like one speaks with a lover or a doctor, though he was not a doctor. He told her that when he was imprisoned in Russia, it was just in his last year of studies and he was almost a doctor, and when he got out of jail he left everything behind and immigrated to Zion, where no medical school had yet been opened. And thus he compromised and became a bacteriologist. But in Gaga's eyes he was a full-fledged doctor, and she called him Dr Yankinton, and the name stuck with his acquaintances and eventually the neighbours as well. And even his colleagues in Balfour-Hadassah Hospital, where he worked, called him Dr Yankinton, and he walked down Balfour and Mazeh Streets in a white coat.

Gaga cleaned all her garments, save her shoes, with soap and water every evening, and therefore tended to go to bed late, at one or two in the morning, and went around the next day exhausted. One could not tell her age by looking at her. Neighbours said that she was an old woman who had disguised herself as a young woman, while her students said that she was a young woman who looked like an elderly one. Indeed, her head was always encased in her black wig, which covered her forehead with thick bangs, and her eyebrows were also black and thick.

Every Friday before the rest of guests arrived, Gaga would visit Mr Yankinton in his office, and this went on for years. In those years each would tell his life story to the other, repeating it over and over. Mr Yankinton would tell of his Zionist activities in Russia and his imprisonment under the Tsar, and how he escaped from Russia to Zion, and about his first child who was born here and died of pneumonia when he was 30 days old, and about his medical studies which were cut off. Gaga would respond: They were not cut off, Joseph, they were not cut off. Everything you missed there you have since made up with all the treatments you have given to thousands of people who owe you their lives or at the very least their health. And then she would tell him about her childhood in Russia and the injury to her skull caused by her brother Judah's wildness in those days, and how today he neglects her parents a bit, when all the burden falls on her, and she must wear a wig, which is not a simple matter when it is so hot outside, but at home she uses a fan. Mr Yankinton, who had never needed either fans or heaters, and also forbade his family to use them, issuing the command as a high-level medical order, thus bringing on his daughter no fewer than five or six lingering colds every winter, simply said: Gaga, you blame yourself too much. You don't need it. But Gaga, who had already tried to rid herself of the big fan which served her faithfully in all the bedrooms and in the kitchen when she prepared her daily salad, but brought it back into service after seven days because she could not stand the suffering, simply said: But Joseph, it's because of the wig, and Mr Yankinton forgave her because he understood that she had an additional trouble, unique to her, beyond the normal human ration of suffering.

How wonderful were those hours between four and six every Friday, and how precarious their existence, for when the hour of six arrived and the first of the friends began to arrive for the weekly get-together—Gaga herself played the mandolin and sang harmony in a few of the songs of the underground, so that by public consensus she was considered an active and essential member—the two began to prepare themselves to part. Mr Yankinton moved his upholstered chair slightly and Gaga stirred uncomfortably on the couch. Then they both rose. Neither of them ever said, We'll see each other next week at the same time, but that is exactly what they were both planning to do, and they would do so until Mr Yankinton crumpled to the pavement of Mazeh Street with intense stomach pains which prevented him from walking any futher. But every meeting was the last meeting, and afterwards, when it became clear that even so there would be another, it was a complete miracle in their eyes, for only thus could they express their faith in the love they felt for each other. Thus years passed, and with them all the great events which happened in the world around them: the State was founded, Jaffa was conquered, Etzel was disbanded and reformed, Jabotinsky's bones were about to arrive in Israel, and many other events, some even amazing and unique, but it was as if none of these things existed during those two hours a week, and when they ended Gaga would go into the kitchen and ask Mrs Yankinton: Can I help? And when she was told no, she would retire to a side room and take up her mandolin to practice a little before the meeting.

I left the Yankinton home as it was getting dark. Over my head loud voices sounded. Just then someone started singing the African song of the underground:

> Everything is a dream to me
> The jungle and all the animals
> And the chorus sings:
> Mombasa, Mombasa,
> The train has already gone in there,
> Armed, armed
> All the Black people are armed

Then the mandolins joined in. Down on the street I began to run. I remembered how Zalman the Thick-bearded, who always came dressed in khaki—with two clothespins stuck to his trousers—lifted me once and seated me before him on his rusted bicycle seat and thus bore me, at my grandfather's command, to my parents' home. My grandfather instructed him to do so and I clung to life and to Zalman's sweaty hands. I so wanted to stay alive then and here my grandfather had decreed my death sentence. I continued to run and circumvented the faltering gait of a heavy woman who had already stopped me on a similar Friday with the words: Child, let me lean on you, it is so hard for me to walk. And I, who was soft-hearted in those days and had also

read the moralistic story about little Chana and her
Shabbat dress, who did not begrudge her new, white
dress, and helped an old charcoal man to drag his heavy
sack of charcoal while she was on her way to Friday
evening dinner at her parents' home, and all the charcoal stains on her new dress became sparkling stars, and
on that same day when it was getting dark, the faltering
woman leaned on me, and the more she praised me for
my good heart, the harder it became for me to tolerate
her excessive closeness, and the smell rising from her
clothes which was not like any other smell, and each
time she would lean on me too heavily, and she led me
on her way, which was not the way I needed to go to get
to my parents' home, where they were waiting for me to
start dinner, and at a certain point she turned towards
Rothschild Avenue until she passed my grandfather and
grandmother's house which, to my utter amazement,
she also recognized and proceeded to disparage them,
speaking their names mockingly.

And I did not have the heart to leave her to herself
and run to my waiting parents. Only later did I find out
that the woman behaved this way with all the children,
and on Friday evening she would always wait for innocent young passers-by, intending to lead them away
from their parents' homes and thus from the real good
deed, and therefore this time I continued to run without
looking to the right or left, lest I meet that woman again
and she would call after me: Child! Child! And those
cries would follow me as I ran since I would not turn

my head. Thus I arrived home and my parents just looked at me with amazement. My father asked: What happened? Did you forget that you have a family?

At the Tel Aviv Zoo, my aunt, my father's sister, chose a monkey who struck her as more intelligent than the rest, since his expression reminded her of a cardiologist who had treated her in Ichilov Hospital, and she thought to encourage us to develop a liking for him as well. This idea followed naturally from her belief that the world held nothing more pure, transparent or impartial than animals of all kinds, and if we learnt to like even one of them, we would increase our chances of having full, rich lives as adults. My aunt also believed that every set of parents with only a single child must hurry to produce a second child, so that after their death, their single son or daughter would not remain alone without a close relative in the world. In her eyes, marriage was a contract which could be broken, and sometimes had to be broken, but the parent–child relationship could never voluntarily be dismantled. A brother will never betray you, so she said, nor a pet.

But our parents did not want to hear a word about pets. At the dinner table, we were forbidden to bring up the subject, except for goldfish or silkworms. Those we had already tried, and would have been permitted to raise them again, but we were no longer interested in those creatures. My sister sometimes tried to circumvent the ban with an appeal to my parents' sense of compassion, for example: On my way home today, I saw a kitten who was so tiny and cute, I think it was hit by a car because it seemed to be limping; or: I saw a little puppy searching for its mother, so small and sweet, indicating with her fingers how little the puppy was. Inevitably my father's face darkened right away as he ruled: No animal is going to enter this house as long as I am alive! Given this barrier, my aunt decided, considering the happiness which would touch our future lives with animals' help, to take us on more frequent visits to the Tel Aviv Zoo. We'll watch the behaviour of Georgio, the intelligent monkey, and get to know him up close, she proposed, as she equipped herself with candy, sugar cubes and rice sticks. After three such visits, Georgio the monkey already welcomed us with a shriek of joy. —He knows us! He knows us! I rejoiced, and my sister, being of a more scientific, critical bent, corrected me: He cannot *know* us, he recognizes us. Georgio caught the sugar cubes (now joined by bananas) and climbed with his stash to the top of the wire fence, just under the roof of the cage. There he sat down and rapidly consumed everything my aunt had produced from her bag. I noticed that he never shared his food with another monkey and never ate slowly and calmly but always at great speed, all the while looking to the right and the left like the bodyguard of a minister or senior official, lest someone nearby might be hatching a plot to steal his meal. And though Georgio was ultimately robbed and tormented, it was in such a way that he could not have foreseen. The next time we came to the zoo, with most of the summer holidays still ahead of us, though there were already fewer visitors at the zoo, just as the days left in our holidays were dwindling, my aunt brought with her an unusually large load, for she had also bought apples this time, thereby provoking the inevitable criticism from my mother, though she never said it to my aunt's face, and perhaps her words contained a grain of envy, since 'buying fresh apples for a monkey, that's something I will never understand'. My aunt bought fresh apples in season, meaning those which had never seen the inside of a refrigerator, certainly not those which had been stored under refrigeration since last summer. Indeed, if she had bought fresh apples but ones which were slightly overripe or old, thus lightly spoilt, my mother would have taken it more calmly, but my aunt could never buy fruit that was even slightly spoilt or had spent time, even one day, in a refrigerator, and considered refrigerating fruit and then selling it as fresh, and even the very act of refrigerating fruit, a sign of the first step on the road to social corruption, which continued with the new lordly behaviour of bank clerks, announcing the rise of a new rank of rulers. As a result, when we arrived at the zoo this time, we were no longer allowed to visit the intelligent monkey. The cashier, who recognized us, said: Yossi requested that I do not allow you into the zoo any more. —Not even if we pay? my aunt asked, beginning to realize that things were not looking good for her, and I asked: Who is Yossi? The cashier said that he was sorry, but after our last visit, one of the monkeys had developed intestinal illness, and other visitors attested that we were bringing food for the monkeys. —Is that forbidden? my aunt wondered, and the cashier eyed her scornfully. Our punishment was limited to this expression of lack of faith by the zoo management, and a ban on entering the Tel Aviv Zoo until the end of the summer. But by the winter we had almost forgotten Georgio. The rain struck the windows and the gutters and we had to wake up too early every morning, which always caused me to regret my habits and my frivolousness which prevented me from going to bed early the night before. Every morning I promised myself that I would never go to sleep so late again, and thus, my aunt's good intention sunk beneath the nightly and daily troubles, her intention to ease my and my sister's future struggles against loneliness by befriending animals.

But during that winter something strange happened. The newspapers reported of a monkey who had escaped the Tel Aviv Zoo. It happened shortly after the Hanukah holiday. That day, in the newspaper which my father brought home, I read about a monkey who crossed King Solomon Street and began to climb the ficus trees planted the length of the pavement. According to the article, citizens called the police and reported in panicked tones that the monkey was apparently overcome by the intoxication of freedom, and now threatened their wellbeing. The article ended by condemning the director of the municipal zoo and his assistant. I remembered how the cashier told us in the director Yossi's name that from that moment on, we were banned from the zoo until the end of the summer, and the scornful glance he turned on my aunt when she asked whether we could enter, like all other citizens, upon purchasing an entrance ticket. When it was all over, my aunt took us to a nearby cafe which had then opened on Keren Kayemet Avenue, where one could read foreign newspapers which were threaded into a long strip of wood through a narrow crack intended for this purpose, even though it did not actually make it more comfortable to hold the newspaper while reading it, and we looked at pictures of dolphins and old steamships and actresses familiar to me from my days of collecting Artistes. My aunt ordered two glasses of iced chocolate and a cappuccino for herself, and told us that she was about to marry a man who had been married three times, and three times had banished his wife from his house, and he made his living writing poetry and translating Russian stories. But, she said, he is older than me and has glasses with yellow frames. After that she waited a little and we drank our iced chocolate, for we had already eaten all the whipped cream off the top with our spoons, making slurping noises, and my aunt waited a moment and said, Maybe they are pink, the glasses. Then she asked: Should I marry such an old man? We did not think then about Georgio the monkey, and in the following winter days we thought of him only rarely. And only now, looking at the newspaper headline, I remembered the monkey. Only the next day did I find out,

when many people repeated the story to me with amazement, that a daring policeman had climbed the ficus tree
where the monkey hung from its crown, and thrown a
fishing net over him—all the police officers enlisted in
this mission had been equipped with such a net—and
thus the monkey was returned to the Tel Aviv Zoo and
the director and his assistant were fined for causing
trouble for the police and wasting public funds by their
negligence. But two weeks later the story repeated itself:
a monkey escaped a second time from his cage at the Tel
Aviv Zoo. The newspaper did not state clearly whether
it was the same monkey who had executed the first
escape. But the second monkey—if it was in fact a different one—bypassed the temptation of the ficus trees
adorning the pavements of King Solomon Avenue, and
without displaying the joy or intoxication which he had
previously exhibited according to the citizens' testi-
mony, headed directly for the flats of people along the
street. In the end he climbed onto the gutter of one of
the old buildings and stopped next to an open window
of a kitchen which, like all kitchens in those days, contained a small table and on it a kilogramme of sugar, part
of it in a jar and part of it in an open dish, somewhat filthy,
with a package of breadsticks and two black bananas
next to it. The monkey did not break into the kitchen,
however, for a police officer—not the outstanding officer
with the net from the previous event—pointed a pistol
at his back and shot him, and the monkey fell from the
third floor of the building to the ground and was killed.
This time the newspaper article ended by speculating

that the monkey escaped from the zoo because he was hungry, and again, if only indirectly, the director and his assistant were accused of stinginess and starving the animals. Looking back, these two articles left their mark on the city's life; people discussed the two monkeys at length—general public opinion held that there were two different monkeys and not just one, even though subsequent events indicated the opposite to be more likely, for once the 'second monkey' was killed, the newspapers did not report any more escapes of monkeys from the Tel Aviv Zoo. This was not real proof, but I myself had no need of proof, for I knew that it was the one and only Georgio the Monkey who had tried to escape twice in a row, two weeks apart, for he missed the portions of sugar and bananas and rice candies which my aunt brought him, but mainly, he had learnt to love people who spoiled him so much that he concluded, of course mistakenly, that it was good and proper to love all people, and thus again made a mistake. My aunt, who wanted to save me and my sister from the lives of loneliness which awaited us, as they awaited every person, and tried to bring us close to the monkeys' world, in the end, all unwittingly, brought disaster to the monkey whom she had chosen for us. Although she had chosen the monkey because of his likeness to the doctor from Ichilov, and because of human beings' fundamental closeness to all monkeys—two reasons which do not contradict each other—in the end, she brought on her chosen monkey a life of loneliness and suffering which began with inchoate longings for certain humans and ended with an expression of complete faith in all humans, and disaster. I began to miss Georgio the Monkey again during the boring hours of school, in the central sewing rooms, watching the needle diving again and again into the blue pieces of fabric which bunched up in my hands, against my will, while outside heavy drops of rain washed the roofs and gutters, and I remembered the hot sunny days, walking into the zoo alongside my aunt and sister, and felt the painful weight of the past.

That winter my father began to take lessons in English and driving. This was the beginning of his miraculous year, a year whose likes he would never see again in his life. And even though it seemed that nature was kind to him that year—it did not continue to be so kind in the following years. But my father could not know this then, and when the columns of profits began to replace the columns of losses in his business ledger, my father decided to take steps to improve the family's quality of life. First, he bought himself Radak's commentary on the Book of Psalms, printed on parchment rather than paper, as they used to do 200 or more years ago, and then purchased Ibn Ezra's commentary on the Torah, and then informed us of the glad tidings that once a week, on Fridays, we would begin to receive one book of our choice. My father kept this agreement for one year before he had to cease because the balance of profits in his business became poor again and even began to deteriorate. But that year, we would come home from school on Fridays one and a half hours late, to my mother's relief, since it meant she could be one and half hours late to finish preparing lunch, for she never managed to stick to a timetable, and in some miraculous way would keep up a tranquil facade whenever my father threw her looks of disappointment and despair, or looks meant to push her to action, which anyway all meant: What will be? And: How did you get into this situation anyway? And thus it was also when he invited guests for the Seder meal, for it was impossible to begin the ceremony and ritual until the main course was fully heated up on the small kerosene burner which burned constantly on a low flame, and the potatoes were not soft yet. Faced with such delays, my father's gaze would always express powerlessness and defeat, while the guests would be milling politely about the festive rooms and murmuring: it's OK, no big deal, and thinking in their hearts: What kind of wife did poor Mr Biederman marry . . .

But during the miraculous year, my mother had some space to breathe. We returned from the bookshops about an hour and a half after all the schools in the city had closed on Fridays, that is to say, at 3 in the afternoon. Sometimes we chose our books from the 'Yesod' shop, at the corner of Allenby and Gruzenberg streets. When we did not find the book we hungered for at that moment, we crossed the street towards Mogrebi and

entered 'Yavneh'. There we were welcomed by a woman
whose voice was low and authoritative, though not
unpleasant, who did not move from her place at a narrow desk, almost touching the crowded bookshelves,
piled with papers and pencils. This wise woman, without leaving her paperwork, served us attentively as
though she nurtured a special affection for my father. In
the Yavneh shop, my sister chose for herself *With the Rod
of the Nations,* and a week later *The Settlers on the Mountain*
by Rivka Alper, and I chose *Youth Flies towards the Sea* and
This is the Story of Dan, and the books of Bibi, which
included two volumes of Bibi alone, and two volumes
of Bibi's great journey, in an artistic edition, and when
Karni's birthday came around, I asked my father's advice,
for I did not know how to choose a book that would
please her. My father suggested poems by Aaron Zeitlin,
and the book was purchased and inscribed with affectionate words from me. I had great faith in my father's
choice, but Karni, who had never thrown away a gift
in her life, kept the book closed, just as it had been
given to her, for decades on her crowded bookshelf, and
never opened it except for the page with the inscription
which was opened and read on her birthday, in my
father's miraculous year. Months later, when my birthday arrived, I asked for *The Family and the Free Child*—a
book on what was then called free education, of whose
existence I had learnt by reading the newspaper. My
father's face fell when he heard my request, but an agreement was an agreement. In the end, I received the book,
bearing a somewhat forced inscription: 'Wishing you a

happy birthday, this book was purchased at our daughter's request.' In the second half of the miraculous year, I joined my father on an expedition to buy a birthday present for my mother. In those days, there was already no reason to hurry on our shopping trip, for choosing our books in the Yavneh shop had become almost effortless, since, without moving from behind her desk, the wise saleswoman with the deep voice guided us wonderfully through every corner of the shop, saying: Take the ladder, child, lean it against the tall left-hand column and you will see all of Mark Twain there. But check at the end of the row also, *Huckleberry Finn* should be there. Without getting up, she knew unerringly the location of every book. Meanwhile, my mother, who had become accustomed to the new lunch hour, which was no longer new to her but had become a routine reserved just for Fridays, began to fall behind again, and we, who usually came home at 3, discovered that once more we had to wait an hour or an hour and a half until the potatoes were soft and the slices of onion browned a little more, until they took on their proper golden colour.

And thus, on that Friday which was near my mother's birthday, when we had finished choosing our books, we continued on in the direction of Herbert Samuel Street, to the gift and souvenir shop, six or seven steps down from street level. Not more than two or three hours remained until the start of the Shabbat, but my father, who did not want to rush my mother on her birthday, conversed at length with the shopkeeper, and after discussing the results of the Peel Commission for

Arabs and Jews concerning dividing the Land of Israel, compared to the United Nations proposal of 1947, my father hesitated for a few moments but finally chose the object on which he had already set his heart. It was a silver cigarette case with two layers of engraving. Inlaid over a layer of delicate filigree strands, engraved the width of the case, was a map of the whole Land of Israel from Dan to Be'ersheba. It was an elegant case which could be placed casually on the table before guests arrived, and then opened as if by chance, so that the wooden lining would appear next to the cigarettes lying tranquilly side by side as ambassadors of a world of leisure, and the guests would observe all this and take a cigarette if they felt like smoking. Of course this gift imposed a certain obligation on the hosts, to ensure that the stock of cigarettes was renewed in a timely fashion so that the box would be ready for the guests at any moment. My father took this task upon himself, while my mother, to whom the gift had been given, was only required to admire the box's beauty, examine the borders of the map of Israel, and receive pleasure from all this. My mother, incidentally, had never smoked in her life.

The miraculous year came to a close. My father, who had received several driving lessons from the teacher recommended by Guri, the wealthy brother-in-law, and had toyed with the thought of buying a small family car, ended his lessons before the year was out because he understood that his money would not cover both what the driving teacher demanded and also the price of the car itself, and it would be pointless to fulfil only one of these original aspirations without the other. Immediately afterwards, he also ceased his English lessons, after receiving 20 lessons from a man whose doleful expression declared: What is the point of being alive, and what do I care how this Jew progresses in his knowledge of English, since anyway he will never develop a correct accent and he will continue to say 'Vashington' and 'Vrong number'. The teacher was therefore let go and my father began to panic that his business was frozen for the meantime, while his money had run out. Thus his miraculous year came to an end.

In those days when I became addicted to sorrow over the death of Georgio, the wise monkey, while the fear this death stirred up, which could perhaps have justified it in some way, became less and less comprehensible to me, my father brought home a rival for us. He was the son of my mother's poor cousin, poorer than us, whose husband worked in the Tel Aviv wholesale market, sealing cartons of fruits and vegetables with metal rods and a hammer. This job, the cousin told us at one of the rare occasions where the entire family gathered, that is to say, at weddings and funerals, does not suit Arush, for he has had no strength at all ever since the war ended, and what little strength he has left is not enough to lift that heavy hammer all day and bend metal rods. When Guri, the wealthy uncle, tried to suggest that Arush might protect his delicate hands by wearing gloves, and told of how, on his last visit to South Africa, he saw the white landlords who worked on a farm protecting their hands with gloves, while supervising the black labourers who were doing the dirty work, my mother's cousin listened politely to his thesis, though she did not understand it, except to sense that it was somehow directed against her and her husband Arush, until she finally broke in: But Arush never *wanted* to wear gloves. You don't think I told him to? He has been refusing to listen for 10 years already.

As to my mother's poor relatives, not a few hold the opinion that they are actually not poor at all, and that Arush does not bend metal bars in his job at the wholesale market but, rather, bends thin tin strips which a child could bend easily without a hammer, and that in his free time he is looking into acquiring two empty lots in the Holon sand dunes, which are the bright new promise in the real-estate market, and though today he lives in poverty with his wife and two sons in a small basement flat on Bogroshov Street, all that is on account of his stinginess, since he has decided to wait until the man subletting the flat's third room—an elderly man with one foot in the grave—with whom Arush signed a key money agreement in a moment of weakness or misplaced emotion, would die, and then the room would revert to Arush's possession and once more rejoin the proper layout of the original flat. —The flat would then become itself again, so Arush explained his financial situation and his hope to others, and at the same time thought of how he would then build the plaster wall which he had been planning during his nights when worry banished sleep from his eyes, and how he would improve his lot by joining the abandoned porch to the living room. But the old man did not die. It seemed that he was actually refusing to die, and begun inventing tricks to outwit death, such as exercising and deep breathing at sunrise in Meyer Park, according to an Indian method, and almost endless rapid walking from King George Street and even further, and in addition to all this, moderate consumption of fruits and vegetables with no eggs or meat. All these changes did the old man good, and he already did not look as old as he did on the day he signed the rental contract with Arush, but they were bad for Arush, whose appearance and physical upkeep steadily weakened until he ceased visiting the Hapoel Sports Club of which he was once so enamoured when he prided himself on his fitness and rowed in a boat on the Yarkon River. But while Arush and his wife, my mother's cousin, were busy with issues of livelihood and property, their son Aryeh's performance in school deteriorated, and the boy's mother, my mother's cousin, was invited to the next parents' day, for by then the teachers had already given up trying to speak with the father Arush, who would always react in the same way to their words of constructive criticism about his son, yelling: If Aryeh is not listening in class, then perhaps it is not interesting enough! At school they concluded that the father was an uncommunicative type from the Diaspora, while the son's poor performance raised the possibility that he would soon be expelled.

From the day of that parents' meeting, Aryeh began showing up regularly at our house to prepare his homework under my father's tutelage. My father felt that he had to save Arush, called thus by our family because of the similarity of his name, Aryeh, to his father's name, Aaron, and the fact that both names could adopt the same nickname. If no one helps Arush, what will happen to him? my father asked. If they expel him from school, he will end up on a kibbutz, perhaps even Kibbutz Geva. Kibbutz Geva had a bad name with my parents, who felt that one should do everything possible to avoid ending up there. Therefore the boy Arush began arriving every day, whiny with the troubles that had befallen him, exhausted from the burden of life and the weight of his pencil case, frayed on the edges, and he would go directly to the third room with my father on his heels. Books and grimy notebooks piled up on both sides of the desk and my father taught him geography. Here is the sea and here is the dry land. What's the big deal with geography? Here are extinct volcanos, stars, the world. My father wanted to speak only briefly of geography, and then, having fulfilled his obligation, free himself to calculate the column of labourer's salaries by the evening, but Arush pulled out an old exam paper from his pencil case: What is the capital of Turkey? Istanbul. What is the capital of Afghanistan? Kabul the Capital. Which country produces primarily beer? France. What is the capital of France? Dublin. So far, Arush got only one answer wrong. What is the big deal with geography?

After two months of such studies, Arush's grades in geography rose somewhat, a fact which amazed me. But Arush started to like the subject of geography, and in his heart had already changed his former goal, the secret one, to leave the school at the appropriate moment and register for Tadmor Hotelier School, even if he had to wash and dry dishes there and set tables for diners, with the ultimate goal of becoming a famous chef, the likes of which had not yet been seen among Tadmor graduates, for a new goal, to become a geographer and organize a research expedition which would cross oceans and seas in order to dredge up the remains of sunken pirate ships from their bottoms. Although Arush would become a geographic researcher in the end, he would come to forget his dream of dredging up remains of sunken pirate ships, if we ever really forget things that we once aspired to and wanted, but when he got a little older he would be appointed the managing editor of a marine research encyclopaedia which would include the honoured entry 'Pirates'. After that they learnt maths, and my father conducted an experiment in which he followed the footsteps of the deceased Professor Frankel, author of the book *Foundations of Mathematics* and other books, and gave Arush, step by step and in the form of questions and answers, the essence of Pythagoras' theorem, without calling it by name. My father remembered that when he arrived in Israel during the war and deluded himself with the hope that he could study mathematics at Hebrew University, he arranged a meeting with Professor Frankel to ask his advice, since all my father's years of education, until the war broke out, were in cheder and yeshiva, with the sole purpose of understanding the holy texts, but from the day my father consulted with Professor Frankel, the theoretical side of his life underwent a certain change, which did not, however, find outward expression. In the world of actions, my father continued to concern himself with producing wool thread and dyeing it, but he retained the book *Foundations of Mathematics*, which Professor Frankel was good enough to give him as a gift, together with the advice: My child (thus he addressed my father, since at that time my father was a young man, while he, Professor Frankel, was elderly), read the beginning of this book. If you understand everything written in it up to, let's say, page 60, and Professor Frankel mournfully turned the book's large pages until he passed a series of drawings of sharp angles and triangles, and come back and tell me that you understood it—I will accept you immediately to the department. My father read Professor Frankel's book from beginning to end, and despite the fact that he not only understood the text but was greatly influenced by it, becoming most enthusiastic, as though someone had freed him of a great weight which until that moment no one, not even he himself, had noticed, my father did not return to Professor Frankel, for he thought he would be asking too much for himself, and in a poor, washed-out country, as a husband and father to two girls, he could not permit himself to study mathematics in Hebrew University. And even so, a locked door was opened before him, and now he tried to lead Arush through it in a way that he had never tried to lead us. From the ample pages, decorated with drawings and the beautiful shapes of *Foundations of Mathematics*, Arush became acquainted with geometrical theorems and principles of square-root theory which were not required at all by the Education Ministry curriculum, but strangely, his grades on his exams went up so impressively that his math teacher called him in for a meeting.

The only subject my father did not manage to teach Arush was the English language. With textbooks scattered over the wooden desk, my father pulled together what little knowledge he had stored in his brain following the lessons he took with the doleful teacher, and added to this what he remembered on his own from his school days, calling on an English–English dictionary and Bentwich's English–Hebrew dictionary, but these were not enough, and the two would tire quickly and fall asleep sitting up. I passed by in the hallway and saw through the open door how their heads had fallen onto the open books and unfinished assignments.

At a certain point the studies came to an end. Arush was no longer at risk of becoming an external child in Kibbutz Geva, and my father, who wanted to see his one student advance, not only towards a life in which he would acquire as much knowledge as possible, but, at least as important, would develop a proper sense of taste and beauty, equipped him on parting with a selection of books from our old bookshelves. Among them were the four volumes of Bibi and Bibi's great journey, Doctor Dolittle's *Puddleby Adventures*, *Youth Flies over Sea*, Bialik's translation of *Don Quixote* and *The Robinsons Under the Sea*, which I particularly loved and read many times, and every time I reached the description of the reunion with the father, the submarine pilot who went underwater and did not come up for 12 days, and his family who did not recognize him at all at first, since his hair had turned white in those few days, I would burst into loud sobs. When I returned late that day from school, after gym class, and I no longer saw Arush waiting for my father in the third room, but I saw my father lying on the couch, having fallen asleep while reading the newspaper, and our bookcase partially emptied, I understood everything. My father had brought us a rival. And worse: something of his former love for us had to retreat before the intruder, to make room for a new and different love, and mourning that loss took the edge off the pain of losing the books.

But in another year a brother was added to our family. A new baby was born, after my parents no longer wanted to hear of more births, certainly not after the terrible war and after such a long break, but then a pregnancy at 39 took my mother by surprise, and it was, like the lucky number of a gambler who never won—a boy. Suddenly happiness, something which had not been known in our family, at least not that we had been aware of, flooded us all. My sister was appointed to announce the birth to extended family members, and I heard her calling out loud, after she dialled Uncle Carmi's telephone number, I have a boy! I have a boy! And my father, from the other room, with a smile still on his face, corrected her: I have a brother, I have a brother . . .

But after 10 days my parents decided to send me to a farmhouse in Ramata'im to make things easier for my mother as she adjusted to the difficulties of a new life which in many ways had changed so as to be unrecognizable. I travelled with my father by bus to Ramata'im, a village whose single street was bisected by the intercity highway, with old farmhouses on both sides of the street. The place chosen for me was a farmhouse built on the edge of the village, with a path leading to a low hill planted with orchards. I did not ask how my parents, who never showed any interest in farm life and never had contact with any farmer for all the time they had been in Israel, discovered the existence of the farmer from Ramata'im whose family took me in, as agreed, for 20 days in a row, since children, as had been inculcated in me early on, were not allowed to ask themselves such questions. Only later did I surmise that my parents were advised by a close relative who had undergone a similar experience, and also sent his daughter to a farmhouse in Ramata'im so that his wife could recover her strength in preparation for returning to normal life.

I travelled to the farmhouse with my father by bus. My father held a small suitcase, black, into which my mother had folded a few garments for me: pyjamas, extra

shoes and a sweater for cool evenings. This was the first
time I had ever slept away from home, and I would be
obliged to sleep in this place alone.

Although in the end I stayed in their house for 14
days, I did not get to know the Ramata'im farm family's
way of life up close, nor farm life in general. The farmer's
children were already grown. But the neighbour's
daughter, a girl named Atida, volunteered or perhaps
was paid to befriend me. We did indeed become friends.
But this friendship ended when the 14 days were up,
leaving a residue of longing in my heart. For years I
looked for a girl, and afterwards a young woman and
then a mature woman, named Atida. It was an unusual
name even then, and I convinced myself that if I met
someone in the course of my life with that name, it
would be the Atida who was my friend during those two
weeks when it befell me, without my understanding
why, to live among strangers and to feel that I had no
one except her. But I have already lived out most of my
days, and I have yet to meet a woman by that name.
Meanwhile, the tormented yearning has long since
receded, yielding to a mild curiosity which too has eventually faded to the background, together with all the
heart's fears of distant meetings.

Atida used to come to the farmer's house every
morning and stay with me for the entire day, returning
to her parents' home only at nightfall. First we would
walk to the farmer's large chicken coop, from which I
had been ordered to collect the new eggs which the
hens had laid in the early hours of the morning. The

hens had special laying compartments all to themselves, and somehow knew that they were required to lay their eggs in them. Though they did it in the same way that humans defecated, only humans do so in toilets. Some of the eggs still radiated the body warmth of the mothers who had not actualized their motherhood. I held onto those eggs longer than the rest and rubbed them gently with my palm so that their heat would not dissipate quickly. We placed the eggs in a carton lined with hay, and thus ended our day's work. From then on we wandered about the village. We watched a film, we picked apples from the orchard on the hill. Above us were blue skies and clouds in the shape of sailboats that floated away to nowhere. Atida revealed to me her secret: when she grew up, she would live in a kibbutz and raise a girl whom she would call Rose of Sharon. When Rose of Sharon would be a young woman, Atida would teach her the names of all the flowers and trees in the world and the names of all the animals who live in Israel. But in the evenings Atida was gone. I sat in the farmer's house, surrounded by strangers who spoke among themselves in an unintelligible language. The farmer's wife opened the door to the balcony which was also the veranda to the yard and people—including neighbours from adjacent houses—occupied every possible seat, enjoying their short rest hours before the next day's labour. The farmer's wife served hot tea in glasses and bowls of dried fruit. The neighbours discussed which insurance policy was the best and most correct when you wanted to preserve an old car. They said: Don't be tempted by ads! They

directed affectionate words towards the new generation
of weather forecasters and praised the 'new style' of
the presentation, and asked each other, What did the
Apel family do to their calves to turn them into milk-
producing cows so quickly? The farmer's son spoke of
an upcoming glider flying competition and told of the
outstanding performance of his youngest son. Above me
was a black sky full of stars. They were not the same stars
that I loved to watch from the porch of my parents'
home in Tel Aviv, nor was it the same sky. It was so foreign and far away, as if Ramata'im were not a 20-minute
ride away from Tel Aviv, even at rush hour but, rather, a
distant settlement which had been prepared for us
without love, a penal colony for military personnel who
were generally obedient but who had been corrupted
and still retained certain seeds of rebellion or sedition,
or of invalids with contagious diseases, among them lep-
rosy for which a cure had already been found in the
wide world but here they had not heard of it, or of crim-
inals who grew old in isolation behind thick walls and
no longer posed a danger to the public though their
punishment was not yet exhausted and they still had to
bear it to its end, or of brave settlers who had landed on
a desolate planet, spearheading a settlement which in
due time would take in all the refugees from Earth. I
watched all these scenarios. They were figments of
my imagination, and a sharp pain passed through my
body and remained as witness to future days which
would take the place of this day, in which, then as now,
the most precious thing would be just that which was

lacking, and as such it would thicken within me, more confident than what exists and more tangible than the spirit can absorb.

Three times during this period my father came to visit me and seemed to me like someone coming to visit a prisoner or a soldier in boot camp. Three times he finished his workday early at the factory or the sales office, and skipped lunch to board a bus which left from the Central Bus Station to Sharon. On these three occasions he told me how the baby brother was progressing surprisingly for his age, and his gaze on the world was very focused, and how my mother was resting now and recovering her strength after the difficult birth, and how my sister was helping her with everything and becoming a real little mother at her side. And I, as an experienced farm girl, led him to the black hens' laying compartments and to the grapevines climbing on the pots which were originally hung for growing vegetables for home use, before the farmers changed their minds, and I showed him the flat holes created by rats—one night, I saw two of them fighting in the shadow of the large dining table—and then I walked him to the intercity highway. He still seemed to me to be a messenger from another world, who now had to return to that world, and at the bus stop, until the bus arrived, I waited until it grew dark and the stars of Ramata'im appeared in the black sky.

Many years have passed since those moments, spans of time which we arrange for ourselves in almost equal lengths, to make it easier to tell ourselves our life story, and always from the end to the beginning, and thus I came to understand only later, future periods of time would never witness such feelings as those I experienced waiting next to my father at the bus stop on the intercity highway, in the chill of approaching evening, with crickets' tedious voices floating to me from the fields until the sky grew black.

Two days had not yet passed since I had last accompanied my father to the bus stop, and the farmer approached me: Child, he said with a gentleness which took me by surprise, we are bringing you home to your house, Papa called and said that Mama is ill and that it is better for you to be near her. —Mama is ill? Better for me to be near her? I did not understand much, but I still understood that which was worse than anything. The joy which burst in me at his first words, 'We are bringing you home,' lasted no longer than the words hanging in the air of the room, and immediately after that was replaced by the sinking of 'Mama is sick,' and the farmer, who could not tell me anything more than what he had already said, accelerated his pickup truck towards Tel Aviv. When I mounted the steps of the building on George Eliot Street, I detected a medicinal smell wafting from the closed door of my parents' home, and the farmer, still by my side, asked from the entrance: So what happened so suddenly, Mr Biederman? And my father brought us into the third room as though we were guests and asked, Will you have some tea after your journey? And my father said: An accident, she had a car accident. Then he turned to me: How are you feeling? And I had been remembering on the way home my dead grandfather and grandmother, and how I returned home one day and saw that my parents' dinner was left on the kitchen table, the congealed soft-boiled eggs leaving yellow holes, and an upturned chair lying there, which was perhaps the hardest thing to see, since panic clung to this place and remained in it from the moment the doctor rang the doorbell wildly and called my father and mother, knowing that this would be the end of the man who was my grandfather who, when I was a small child—after giving me tea and home-made jam and begging me to drink and eat, and teaching me how to take a bite of the thick jam and at the same time swallow the tea in little sips like the Russians, and singing the national anthem for me and making sure that I repeated his voice, words and tune, and pronounced all the words precisely and separately—commanded Zalman, in his khaki with clothespins on the hems of his trousers, to take me home on his bicycle, and my soul fluttered between life and death the entire way home. And then I remembered Sonia Knizhnikov who fell into her illness and had not left her place by the window since, and was becoming smaller and smaller, and each time I came to the house on Yavneh Street I looked at Sofa's window and there was her mother sitting next to the window looking out at the street, smaller than she had been at my previous visit.

I was relieved when I heard that my mother was hurt in a car accident. Just a car accident, I told myself, a car accident and not a terrible disease which takes over the body and cannot be expelled. I rejoiced that my mother would recover quickly from the accident and then would forget that she was ever struck by a black car which zoomed by while she was still in the middle of the road, totally oblivious, and struck her lower back. My father said that my mother had to rest now. He told us, we have hired a nanny to watch over your baby brother and over you two, so that Mama can rest. The doctor said that only rest can help my mother now, and if she had not been so distracted, thinking all the time about her children, and suddenly, on her way back from the greengrocer with the rattan shopping bag in her right hand, in the middle of the road, remembered that she forgot to buy vegetables for soup, and turned on her heels, and the driver of the black car could not have known that she was going to do that. Right? He could not have predicted that you would have a mother who is so busy thinking about her children's welfare. Right? And she turns around in the middle of the street to buy you vegetables for your soup, and he runs over her, and the family doctor now indicates with his hands a motion of rising up and thumping, Tach, Tach! And the woman falls on the road and the ambulance arrives within a minute, of course, since she fell a minute's walk away from the ambulance station, and they take her to the hospital, and it's true that she needs to rest and it's very good that you hired a nanny, but whose fault is it all? And what were you doing while your mother was lying on the road? the doctor turned to me, I didn't see you there! And who collected the items that were scattered from her wallet, lipstick and rouge and a cotton ball? It was hard not to conclude that the doctor was accusing us outright, all members of the family but particularly my sister and I, and mainly me, for my mother's injury and the accident which caused it. I fled to the big room, wanting to see my mother, to kiss her hands and beg her to forgive me. My mother stroked me a little through the haze of painkilling medications she had been given. I asked her if she had forgiven all of us for the soup vegetables and for my not being here, but she, through the pain which was subsiding, and the concern for the new baby and the fear of what was to come—was able to see me only with the part of her which brought her calm, and therefore answered, with her hand still enclosed between my two hands: Now I will sleep a little.

My father hired a girl named Aliza to take care of the family, and life returned almost to its former groove. Aliza was full of energy, quickly taking charge of the housekeeping, including caring for the baby. She arrived every morning at 7.30, dressed in a clean white blouse and full skirt, and her brown hair was chestnut, pulled partially to the side beyond her natural part, which during working hours was hidden by her hair's curly fullness. We were in a great hurry, too much of a hurry, to accustom ourselves to the presence of this twenty-three-year-old girl whose blue eyes and pleasant smile, dazzling white, only increased our wonder at her efficiency and organizational skill, for Aliza, unlike my mother, would tackle several different tasks at once; while she was setting up the small cauldron for boiling diapers on the fire, she began peeling a large eggplant, and when she had sliced it thickly and washed the slices on a wooden tray which she had found hidden in the depths of a kitchen cupboard, since my mother had never taken advantage of its excellent qualities, and pressed the eggplant with a little salt—she watched over the pan of milk which she had set on the gas burner earlier for our tea, and meanwhile took out soft cheese and vegetables from the refrigerator for breakfast, and throughout all this activity she spoke incessantly of her husband who was currently on reserve duty in the Army. Incidentally, the whole time she was in our house, 'Aliza's husband' never stopped serving in reserve duty, which was called then 'Atudot', and Aliza was the first to open my eyes to the laws of evil in the world when she told me how worried she was that something bad would happen to her husband, which amazed me, since he was not in combat, but she told me that during each training session, 3 per cent of the training forces were expected to be killed, and everything was included in the Army's calculations and predicted ahead of time, and when I asked whether it was possible to be more careful, she said: Of course not, silly little fool. There is a quota of people who have to be killed. There can't be fewer. They have already tried everything, and the level of training has to be improved all the time. Right? Aliza accepted the possibility that her husband might die in order to improve the general level of training, and this idea, which seemed distant and strange to me at first, approached me slowly over time, like the secret beyond the stories of A *Thousand and One Nights*, in order to say that something impenetrable and therefore evil awaits us beyond the colourful flags and anthems and the bugles sparkling in the sun, and that is the state.

Thus my mother's rival lived and worked in our midst, glowing and more youthful, arriving each morning in clean, pressed clothes, who never forced us to wait an hour or an hour and a half before lunch was served, and still managed to care for the baby, making sure his skin stayed dry and taking him for walks along the avenue, who was always smiling and speaking with longing of her husband who would some day be killed and who did not see a contradiction in this. It seemed to me that my father had also became younger and more vigorous since her arrival. Those days, those very days, saw my true betrayal of my mother, when I, like everyone else in the family, let myself be swept away with great affection for a strange woman and turn it into love.

On one of those days, close to the only Jewish holiday which was observed not by strict prohibitions but only concessions, among them very strange ones, such as the permission for women and men to sit together during prayers, the upcoming Purim holiday inspired us to take part in the prestigious costume competition

scheduled to take place, as it did every year, on the plaza
of the Tel Aviv Zoo. My friend Karni and I were joined
by Etti, a golden-haired girl whose costume—a long,
black dress covered with sparkling cardboard stars,
called 'the Queen of the Night'—was, in my family's
opinion, sure to place in the competition, possibly even
take first prize. Etti was so beautiful in her black dress,
with her golden hair and her blue eyes, the dress which
her mother—the neighbourhood seamstress in daily
life—had sewn for her with elation and inspiration wor-
thy of her first ball, and indeed Etti graced our home like
the scion of the British royal family making her appearance at the home of a poor subject, living in a corner of
the far-flung Empire. Alongside Etti, Karni was dressed
up as a letterbox, a costume dreamt up by Mrs Yankinton,
who saw it as an educational message in a humorous
spirit, as she said, and its execution included an intricate
cardboard hat made of red papier-maché to resemble the
top of an old-fashioned letterbox, the work of Mrs
Yankinton's friends, more talented than she at handi-
work, and a skirt to which filmy scarves had been
pinned, bearing drawings of postal stamps in a rainbow
of colours. Indeed, the idea had burst on Mrs Yankinton
after she had received a set of such scarves, a gift from
an old friend in the Party who had returned from a trip
to Switzerland, and she had spread them out one winter
evening, next to the table in their rather dishevelled
third room, and they had appeared to her, in the lamp-
light flickering because of a flawed bulb, as a much-
desired jewel from foreign lands, the postage stamps

bearing the marks of countries like Thailand and Japan, and then she understood that she had found a costume for her daughter, and by the next day had already begun preparations. Meanwhile, I was dressed as a safari hunter, in too-tight boots, trousers, a short jacket and a green hat bearing a ridiculous green feather, a costume which had also been first thought up in the Yankinton home, and I, lacking a critical faculty, had swallowed the idea whole and carefully completed all the required cultural details, turning to relatives who had arrived at that time from Canada to try out the role of new immigrants, a trial which, however, did not go well, but their closets were stuffed with the strange clothing of the wealthy. Karni and I were like two courtiers who had once served the Queen but been dismissed years ago for committing some indiscretion, and now, as a sign of kindness, permitted to accompany their mistress for one day on her way to her festive appearance at her first ball.

We left for the zoo accompanied by my father, my baby brother and Aliza the nanny. A rather strange procession: a letterbox in rags, a silly-looking hunter and a beauty in a black dress, covered with cardboard stars. And following these three—a happy man in a white straw hat, a young woman in summer clothing and a baby. But no one paid us any attention. The zoo was crowded with visitors, most of them children with a knot of adults surrounding each one, neighbours, parents, grandparents, everyone with happy smiles which said: We're going to win big. But they had not won yet, though their chances looked to me to be 10 times greater than ours. When I saw the spectacular costumes, most of them reflecting the way of life of the last French king's court, before the great Revolution, I despaired, but I still trusted in our Etti's beauty and good luck. A short, energetic woman, a member of the staff running the competition, directed all the competitors to walk, to the sounds of marching music, to a large pen that had been set up at the back of the stage. Five judges sat on the stage, two women and three men, with a pile of pages before them on a long, narrow table, and we stood—separated from all our escorts—in a crowd of other people in costumes, to which we nominally belonged but were only on the outer fringes. I eyed this crowd soberly, like a farmer's daughter who knows that the delicious goose meat now being served on her family's table once belonged to one of the creatures that she fed and cared for on their daily walks under blue skies. We had no chance. But still the place provided a riot of colour, along with a hope dimly tied to Etti's beauty, she who first told us of the blood that flows once a month from the wee-wee of big girls, though I did not understand how such a story concerned us and why it aroused such interest and excitement in my friends, and later she told us that this blood was called 'forty-four' and then, as always when we met in Etti's parents' home, she brought the *Encyclopaedia of Family Health* from her parents' room—two volumes bound in green—and tried to locate the entry 'penis', but nothing was written, and in fact we found no entry like that, and we did not know any other word to search for, and afterwards we paged through to find the word belonging in the same way to a woman's body, something like 'vulva', an ugly, foreign word which no one had ever spoken in our presence, but we believed Etti that this was the correct word, and next to it we did indeed find a detailed description, though unclear what of, and an illustration—a drawing accompanying it, similar to illustrations in textbooks on the human body, with curving lines and tiny numbers referring to a page of explanations. All this was irrelevant to us and did not concern what we were seeking. But Yael Hadar, who was sitting with us, said that it was a woman's sexual organ and that a man inserts his thing there. But first both of them have to undress and lie on the bed, naked, bum to bum, she said, and thus a woman becomes pregnant and a baby comes out. And I, who had once asked my parents how a baby is born, knew that a baby is born from the wedding when the rabbi stands with the bride and groom under the marriage canopy and blesses them, and that everything Yael Hadar said was incorrect. But Yael Hadar even repeated her words and said that her mother and father do this three times a week, bum to bum, and everyone's parents do this, and I did not want to believe her, for this information pained me, and I did not accept that in this ugly way, three times a week, we were all born and our parents were born and I was born and my sister too, and not long ago, not long ago at all, they did it again and my brother was born. I heard the information and did not believe it but I wanted to know, and for a few seconds I accepted the words as though they were true. And thus, despite my aversion, there was something beyond this truth which drew me, and this something, unlike the tempting, appealing aspect which many of us would experience as adults, was supposed to lead us somehow, in a manner that was not entirely clear, towards a change that was inevitably coming to us, against our will. And then Etti brought the book *The Circle* by Arthur Shnitzler and began to read out loud from a section in which the conversants were a soldier and a prostitute, inviting each other to a night of mutual pleasure, and the short lines were arranged in a descending column, like this:

Soldier:

Whore:

Soldier:

Whore:

Each one received something. Each one said something. And we listened in amazement to the impossible in all this and the unbelievable which had touched us once more.

In the meantime, in the large pen set up at the back of the judge's podium of the Tel Aviv Zoo, the number of contestants had grown significantly. I lifted my head so I could breathe better. Blue skies stretched out above me. The day's heat was still at its peak, but I was separated from the sky by a delicate, strong-looking lattice which was somehow familiar. After a moment's thought, I realized that I was under the top of Georgio the Monkey's cage. I looked quickly to the left and right.

Yes, there was the neighbouring herons' cage which extended towards the park. There could be no doubt about it. This was the cage in which Georgio was once imprisoned, in which he passed his days in the human jail and escaped it to die in the end at human hands. And now here I am, between my two friends, seeking a prize from the hands of the jailors' emissaries, and I am not protesting at all; instead, I am slowly approaching the front of the stage. The crowd suddenly thinned out. Without noticing, we had become almost the last ones left, and we mounted the stage in a line, first Karni with her red-letterbox hat already askew, then Etti in her evening gown and at her most beautiful, and finally me, in too-tight boots causing damage which has affected my gait to this day, a blond beard and a hat whose feather had fallen off and gotten lost. But when we passed by the silent row of judges, they were busy with their paperwork. Some of them wrote summaries such as: *The competition went off well on the whole. There were no particular disturbances.* One judge added up the points: 12 +7 - 3 = 16. When it was our turn to pass by, the short secretary of the competition approached the row of judges and whispered something in the ear of the first judge in the row, and he wrote the information on a note which passed from hand to hand. From that moment on, no judge noticed anything but the note which he was about to receive or had just received. Etti's dress did not receive a single point, nor Karni's mail box, except for her strange hat which reminded one of the judges of a letterbox cover which he saw once in an English village, and its appearance stirred him with longing and he gave Karni two points for the hat, but my hunter's garb did not arouse any attention at all. We descended from the stage just as we had mounted it, with no one taking any notice. But when we came down, Aliza was waiting for us with my father and the baby. They shook our hands encouragingly and my father said, almost to himself, Strange, I was sure that Etti would win. A thought came to me—what would Georgio say if my hunter's costume had won? I could not understand why I had accepted Mrs Yankinton's suggestion and put all that work into making myself a costume of a hunter, of all things.

Gradually my mother recovered almost entirely and returned to us emotionally and physically. Aliza left us and we accustomed ourselves once more to the routine of late meals, for which my mother compensated with small meals of citrus fruits and dates or apple and banana or petit-beurre cookies stamped with decorative flourishes, accompanied by orange drink, served to us between meals to satisfy our hunger pangs, and ever since then, we cannot deny our bodies food for as long as we are awake, and we make time for a light meal at any time of day. This is an indecent habit, even though it sprung from only good intentions. When my parents went out for the evening—for they began to go out in the evenings again, primarily to the cinema—my mother would leave a plate next to my bed with plums and chocolate.

Once again my parents left the house and I remained awake. Since I had moved beyond my early childhood years, I had learnt to lie to myself, and I no longer mulled over the question of whether my parents would return or not. I knew that they would return, and I no longer sought the truth. In those days, I found a small job whose main task was to help a girl prepare her homework assignments. From then on, I no longer turned to my parents, who already had difficulty paying the household bills, to cover my expenses. The girl's parents owned a factory which produced ink and typewriter ribbons, two products which would some day disappear rapidly from the world, but this fact did not frighten them. Resourceful as they were, they hurried to retool the machines and became manufacturers of anti-virus programs for computers, thereby moving ahead of their time, at least in Israel. And yet, in the days when they still manufactured ink and typewriter ribbons, and I prepared all their daughter Rina's homework assignments with her except for maths, since that was the subject which I had been unable to grasp since early childhood, Rina's parents hired an additional tutor to teach maths. He was a college student from the History department who understood enough maths to teach a child, daughter of indulgent parents. And while I was finishing my lesson and collecting the few belongings I had brought with me—a pen, a colourful calendar with paintings by Cezanne—my attempt to develop a sensitivity to beauty in my only pupil—and a thick notebook, here came the maths tutor. Indeed, as I left the study room to return home, the maths teacher was just arriving from his home and entering the study room. We met at the entrance and I recognized him as Nati, son of acquaintances of my parents who had accompanied them in their escape from their former homeland during the war, who had been a skinny youth, when I saw him once in his parents' home, sitting next to the stove on a winter day and looking at a picture book, and now he was a student in the Department of General History.

At that time I was reading Leah Goldberg's poems, and more than once whispered to myself the line, 'Then I walked through the world as though someone loves me.' But Nati, the maths tutor, behaved as though he did not see me at all. Our meetings took place every day, five times a week. From Sunday to Thursday we met at the same time and place every day; only on Friday and the Shabbat we did not. The door I exited from was the door he entered by, and sometimes these entrances and exits would occur simultaneously like the timing of stage actors, and other times, while I was still preparing to end my lesson, summing up and adding another word or two, suddenly the maths tutor would be standing next to the closet and I would gather up the few things I had brought with me. See you next time, I would say wordlessly. See you next time, Nati would respond in my mind. And when my parents would go out to visit their acquaintances from the war, I would wait for them to return and not fall asleep. Even when the bus was late or when they returned on foot because they missed the last bus, I would jump up to welcome them when I heard the sound of the key in the door. —How was it? I would ask them, Why did it take you so long, what did they talk about, did they talk about the war again, and was Nati awake, and what year is he in at the University? And sometimes I would not mention him at all in my questions, and I would jump out of bed to see my parents, who only a half-hour ago had seen the house in which Nati grew up, and was a baby like my brother, and now he lived there. And Nati's parents and his house were now the borders which I was allowed to approach and, via my parents, ask indirectly and touch all the things whose independent existence allowed me to pronounce the name Nati or 'the maths tutor' to my weary parents and afterwards to the world. In my heart, I named my upcoming test in my European History class 'Following Nati's time', and throughout the Shabbat I studied articles about the reigns of the great Roman emperors, until the stars came out, and in doing so, like a battalion commander who is being questioned as to whether he heard that his soldiers had been taking booty every time they demolished a house together with its occupants, and he bursts out laughing and says: That's a joke! How can that be? Soldiers in my battalion? For in his heart he knows that it is all true, and it is just as they said, so I knew that on all those evenings when I lay awake and my heart beat for my parents' return, I was not waiting for them but for the maths tutor, and when I heard the sound of the key in the lock, and jumped out of my messy bed to welcome my parents, I did not mean to run to them but, rather, to a stranger, and I hid this fact with my welcoming face. To this day, a chill breeze wafts through my heart when I see once more my ageing parents' shining, grateful faces: You waited up for us again, child? Go to sleep, and in their hearts they are thanking God for their good fortune.

In my dull sewing classes, facing the needles which kept breaking in the machine, I sat in the classroom and heard the shuffle of little feet coming towards us and then passing us slowly. I lifted my head slightly and saw through the window, though already at a distance, my brother's nursery school group. They walked hand in hand, wrapped in little coats and hats on a bright winter day. Roni's nursery school went out every morning to Strauss Park, the nursery school teacher in a short woollen dress, revealing sturdy legs, and the children, with calm feet, like clean silk worms, passing by the tall windows of the Balfour School. These were the days which always gave way to the days of summer heat, burning and unbearably humid, in which my mother, out of a sudden faithfulness to the customs of the former homeland or because of her weakness which had increased with the birth and the accident, decided to spend them in a more pleasant environment. Thus, she took my brother with her to live for a time in the dry climate of the Beit HaKerem neighbourhood of Jerusalem. Each year, my father would escort them to the room which he had already rented for them there, in the house of a local family, and return to us alone. And thus, every day of the week, we, the ones who stayed, would meet in the afternoon hours when my father would return uncharacteristically early from the sales office and take us to a restaurant. There were two places to eat out: Meyer and Jeshurun. The Meyer Diner was tucked away on the second floor of an ordinary residential building on Ahad Ha'am Street, not far from Nachmani Street. Its entrance no different from the entrance to an ordinary residential building: a green door adorned with a small attached knocker shaped like a child's face or perhaps an angel's, but on the other side was a restaurant which had been set up in an old flat whose floor was designed with delicate colours, and it had four rooms. Each room was dotted with chairs and tables covered in white tablecloths, all occupied by patrons at the busy noon hour. Indeed, all the patrons were men in the costume favoured by ultra-Orthodox Jews at that time, that is: black trousers, a black hat, and a worn jacket or black caftan covering a rumpled white shirt.

The waiters were dressed similarly, only without the coat. That would have been impossible to ask of them, to run back and forth on a hot day, with steaming bowls of soup in their hands, wearing a black coat. Though all the patrons sat and sipped hot soup, and all the waiters held up black trays bearing the bowls of scalding hot soup. Incidentally, everyone ate chicken soup with noodles. It was not only the patrons' preferred dish and the specialty of the Meyer Diner, it was the only kind of soup served, lacking any substitute or competition, not here nor anywhere else. I wondered if all these men sent their wives and small children to a summer camp with a more congenial climate, and posters announcing the performance of a guest artist from Tel Aviv, or Israel Yitzhaki and his band, hung on the single board next to Dov's kiosk, between Rishonim Park and the local war memorial, with white pebbles and fiery poppies leading up to it. At any rate, there were no other children in the restaurant. Only my sister and I pressed close to a large table covered with a white tablecloth bearing old stains which had been rubbed out with talcum powder but not removed, and not even fully rubbed out, until the waiter came to take our order, and my father said: Three orders of chicken soup with noodles, since anyway there was nothing else in the restaurant except beef soup with noodles, and we always preferred chicken over beef, perhaps because we soothed our conscience with the thought that slaughtering a chicken to satisfy our hunger cannot be as bad as slaughtering a cow or a bull just to eat its tail, and thus we joined the majority of humanity, since in our hearts we knew that there was no real difference, and the quantity of evil is not measured by the size of the creature we hurt, but rather by how much we cause it to suffer. I remembered as a young child escorting my mother on one of her prolonged shopping trips, until we reached the den of the ritual slaughterer, located where once the few residents of the building who owned cars had parked them, but whose luxury had grown tarnished with time, and my mother, who carried a restless chicken in her hand, turned it over to the ritual slaughterer so that he could kill it for her for the Kaparot ritual, and he carried out the task according to Jewish law and whispered the appropriate verses from Psalms. And when I asked my mother if it hurt the chicken when its soul parted from its body for ever, and did not ask why one needed to kill the chicken at all—a question which would have shown critical thinking and therefore was impossible for a child—my mother answered: It does not hurt him at all. Didn't you see that the uncle slaughterer said a prayer as he picked up the knife? My mother apparently believed in words' power to grant or take away life, as needed, and I accepted her words at face value, and in a certain way I did not ever let those words go, even later in my life. Meanwhile, with part of our childhood already behind us, we sat and slurped from deep bowls of hot chicken soup with large spoons, and our flesh did not burn within us.

But the other restaurant, Jeshurun, was not like the Meyer Diner, nor like any other eatery in the city. It had also once been exclusively Jewish, and even its name testified that it still clung to the Jewish faith, since it bore the secret name of the man who had been first a tribe and then a people beloved by God. All these things were included in the name of the restaurant, and it was a quite a yoke to bear for a down-home restaurant on Mazeh Street off Allenby. The proprietor of the Jeshurun Restaurant sported a black yarmulka on his head, but had given up on other marks of religious faith, and thus, with his hair grown wild, and his thick beard which

covered his face like chunks of cooked cauliflower, he
looked to me like a deity of the desert. With cheap cut-
lery of galvanized tin, on ceramic plates, he served
patrons various flavours of eggplant salad, and this was
the special delicacy which both revealed and hid his
secret in this restaurant which boasted many patrons,
not one of whom wore a black caftan, and most were
labourers who came from the nearby workshops, and
particularly printers and typesetters who worked on the
outskirts of the open-air market and drank dark nectar
from thick glass mugs and supplemented their eggplant
salad with a bit of olive oil, half slices of black bread, and
radishes which were served in a special bowl, only partially sliced, and thus left like a fan or a card shark's deck
which cannot come apart since the cards are artfully
joined at the edges.

 We sat among the many, rather rough, patrons of
Jeshurun Restaurant. Sometimes we arrived first and
had to grab a table before my father arrived from his
sales office, and it was not an easy nor pleasant task to
fight off those who tried to dislodge us—two girls, my
sister in braids in those days—from our newly acquired
territory. The endless questions: Who are you? Where
are you from? What is going on here, two girls taking
up a whole table meant for adults? My sister answered
decisively: Details in the office between two and one!
Meaning: It's none of your business, get out of here. But
in the end we managed to hold on to our spots. One
might say, we were alive, and this was life. Outside the
restaurant on Mazeh Street, where Mazeh crossed Strauss,

opposite the dark Ein Gedi Hospital, Mr Yankinton passed by in a white coat, walking with rapid steps, his long, clumsy legs thrust out to the sides as he walked and his head bent forward and slightly down, with an important stance which said that the pain of those who depend on me, in the end, is my pain. And what do you want, child, he asked when he noticed me, and when will the Queen invite the Princess to play cricket? And further on, Gaga Gorochov carries her musical instrument every Friday afternoon, only to drop it wearily in the corner of the second room on Yavneh Street, and wait for an invitation or perhaps a slightly critical remark from Mrs Yankinton: Go see Osya, he's already waiting for you. And then: Rest a bit there, OK? I'll serve you both tea in a minute. And then, when Mr Yankinton has died, not because he was elderly but because that is the way of every man, Gaga Gorochov still appears, dragging her mandolin on Friday afternoon at precisely the same hour, and passes the time between four and six with Mrs Yankinton, conversing with her as she conversed with her husband twenty years earlier, and follows her into the kitchen when it is time to prepare tea, offering her help. And then she takes the tray and carries it into the second room.

For as long as Mrs Yankinton was alive, Gaga Gorochov did not give up this practice, and arrived for her weekly visit even when all the other musicians and singers of the Underground had long ceased to come, and would converse with her in the same fashion and on the same topics which used to come up incessantly in her conversations with Mr Yankinton. She still spent every evening washing all the clothes she had worn that day, except for her shoes, but now, having retired from her teaching job and subscribed to National Geographic, she knew that she would not find peace until she had visited all the countries whose descriptions appeared in the magazine, accompanied by colour pictures. And until she saw a rickshaw which a man pulled as though he were a horse, and the Buddhist temples and the pagodas in China and Thailand and the glaciers in Lapland and the British Queen's guard, she would not be properly prepared to die. And thus she began to make a list of countries, based on the index of the Brawer Atlas, which was to be found in her house as it was in the house of every teacher in those days, and during her visits to Mrs Yankinton, a new topic was added to their conversations, one which had never come up in the conversations held in that house, on the same day and at the same hours, though not in the same room, nor with the same person. Gaga Gorochov would recount: Lapland—I was there. Czech Republic—I was there. Switzerland—of course I was there. I was in Albania. I was in Norway. I was in Sweden. I was in the Caribbean Islands. The changing of the guard at the Royal Palace— I was there. But there were places and things which she did not mention, and Mrs Yankinton, out of a hidden gentleness whose softness sometimes accompanies old age, held her tongue.

FINIS

Translators' Notes

PAGE 4

three stars to appear | The Shabbat ends on Saturday evening when darkness falls, which is defined in Jewish law as the moment when one can see three stars together in the sky.

Shabbat timer | Jewish law forbids lighting electric lamps on the Shabbat, but it is permitted, before the Shabbat begins, to set a timer which turns them off and on automatically at preset times.

PAGE 5

Ashkenazi | Referring primarily to Jews from Eastern Europe.

PAGE 6

Hassan Bek tower | Referring to the Hassan Bek Mosque, one of the best-known mosques in Jaffa, now part of the Tel Aviv-Jaffa municipality. Built in 1916, it was used by Arab snipers to fire on Jewish neighbourhoods during the months before the British withdrawal from Mandatory Palestine in May of 1948.

PAGE 9

Ze'ev Jabotinsky | A Russian Jewish Zionist leader, author, poet, orator and soldier. He co-founded the Jewish Legion of the British Army in the First World War, and later established several Jewish organizations in Mandatory Palestine, before the founding of the State of Israel in 1948.

PAGE 22

Jaffa Road | A central street in Jerusalem.

PAGE 26

Allenby Street | A central street in Tel Aviv.

PAGE 32

Da'at | 'Knowledge' in Hebrew.

PAGE 36

good for nothing | The Hebrew word is a harsh insult, appearing in the *Talmud*, from the Hebrew root for 'empty'.

PAGE 37

goldies | Shiny foil wrappers from chocolates.

PAGE 43

Flit | A spray insecticide against mosquitos, first invented in 1923 in the US.

PAGE 47

Shikun Vatikim | Shikun is a public-housing development, and Vatikim implies 'first settlers to the area'. Many cities in Israel have a 'Shikun Vatikim', built at the beginning of the State of Israel when housing needed to be erected rapidly for large numbers of immigrants. The word 'Vatikim' can also mean 'old people'.

PAGE 55

Etzel | An acronym of the Hebrew words 'The National Military Organization'. Etzel operated in the British Mandate of Palestine from 1931 to 1948, when it was incorporated into the Israel Defense Forces upon the founding of the State of Israel.

PAGE 61

better for me to die than to live | A citation from Jonah 4:3 'Therefore now, God, take, I beseech Thee, my soul from me; for it is better for me to die than to live.'

PAGE 64

Sholem Aleichem | The pen name (meaning 'Peace be upon you') of Yiddish writer and playwright Solomon Naumovich Rabinovich (1859–1916).

PAGE 66

kibbutz | A collective community in Israel, traditionally based on agriculture. The first kibbutz, Degania, was founded in

1909. Kibbutzim (plural of kibbutz) were originally utopian communities, based on socialist principles.

Palmach | Acronym for 'Striking Forces', the Palmach was the elite fighting force of the Haganah ('Defence'), the underground military force of the Jewish community under the British Mandate of Palestine. With the creation of the State of Israel and its army in 1948, the Palmach was disbanded. Until the creation of the state, there was an ongoing rivalry between the two fighting forces Palmach and Etzel.

Rifle will salute rifle, bullet will fire on bullet | A line from the song 'To the Barricades', lyrics originally written in Yiddish in 1946 by Yossel Kotler.

PAGE 67
Letter from Mama | Lyrics by Israeli poet Nathan Alterman (1910–70).

PAGE 76
Petah Tikva Way | A major thoroughfare in Tel Aviv, now renamed 'Menachem Begin Way'.

PAGE 78
muktze | Something forbidden to touch on the Shabbat.

PAGE 81
Gentile | The author's implication is that if he is light-hearted and playful, he is more like a Gentile than a Jew.

PAGE 83
eve of a holy day | The reference is to the Shabbat. The Shabbat and Jewish holidays start at sunset of the evening before, so the Shabbat begins on Friday evening.

PAGE 86
Queen of the Wilderness | In Hebrew, the word for 'wilderness' is 'tziah' which sounds similar to the name Heitzen.

PAGE 90

Beitar | A Zionist youth movement founded in 1923 in Riga, Latvia, by Ze'ev Jabotinsky, whose goal was to create a modern Jewish state based on the Jews' ancient homeland of Israel, using military force if necessary.

PAGE 91

Pioneers' House | Built in Tel Aviv in 1936 to house young female immigrants.

PAGE 109

Hanukah | An eight-day festival in the Jewish calendar which takes place sometime in December.

PAGE 114

Seder meal | The ritual meal held on the first evening of the week-long Passover festival, at which Jews celebrate their liberation from slavery in Egypt.

PAGE 115

With the Rod of the Nations | A book about the ancient Kingdom of Israel, by Yakov Rabinowitz, published in Hebrew in 1946.

The Settlers on the Mountain | A book about the early Jewish settlement in Palestine, published in Hebrew in 1944.

Youth Flies over the Sea | A children's book originally published in German in 1932 as *Stoffel fliegt übers Meer* by Erika Mann. Hebrew translation published in 1934.

Bibi | A series of children's books originally published in Danish in the 1930s by Karin Michaelis, featuring a girl heroine named 'Bibi', translated into Hebrew shortly after the originals came out.

PAGE 124

external child | A child who did not grow up on a kibbutz but was sent there alone by his or her parents, usually because of financial or other difficulties in the family. An external